A MURDEROUS SUMMER AT BARD

GLENDA RUBY

A MURDEROUS
SUMMER
AT BARD

Library of Congress Cataloguing-in-Publication data is on file
with the Library of Congress

ISBN 978-0-692-93080-9

Manufactured in the United States of America

Greendale Books

First Edition

FOR ROS

A Murderous Summer at Bard

Glenda Ruby

As I look back, now that the deaths are behind us, I realize the problem was right in front of me all summer.

Not *the* problem, but several problems which eventually intersected.

I will lay out the facts.

See if you are able to deduce what was about to happen.

I was not.

INSTABILITY: THE ORDER OF THE DAY

"Don't sell the Basquiat!"

"Don't sell the Basquiat!"

About twenty of us in black tie regalia stood in the O'Connells' entrance hall, shouting objections as our host Franklin announced his intention to de-accession the twelve by twenty portrait of a primitive black head circled with red and gold barbed wire and pictograms. The stunning piece hung on the south wall some ten feet above us.

Franklin shook his head. "Have to. It's unstable."

The *painting's* instability turned out to be the least of our troubles.

That dinner was the first of many such gala evenings during the summer musical festival at Bard College.

If previous festivals' triumphs were accurate predictors of this summer, we were about to enjoy a colorful and amusing succession of chamber music and opera, intriguing archival films, brilliant ballet and modern dance, and marvelously inventive and accomplished stage and orchestral productions.

Alas, had we only known this particular summer would also present a seemingly endless progression of corpses, we might never have left that first evening's security in the old mansion, with its exceptional chef and vast wine cellar.

But none of us knew.

No, that's not correct.

3

A LUNCHEON INVITATION

Occasionally I still make my own frames, doing my bit to keep the Arts and Crafts movement creaking along. As I attached clamps to freshly glued corners, the phone rang.

The dulcet tones of my oldest and dearest friend Huxley Smythe boomed out, "Are you having a rich, productive morning?"

"Indeed, sir!" I replied, wiping traces of wood glue on my jeans.

"I've weeded the asparagus, branded the ferrets, and the soy crop is as high as an anteater's eye. All's well down here in Over Proof Gulch. To what do I owe the pleasure of this interruption?"

"I want you and your fiendishly attractive butler to come to lunch day after tomorrow and meet the new woman in my life."

That stopped me. Huxley, our valley's answer to Rex Reed *cum* Hedda Hopper *cum* Deep Throat, is eighty-something and has been widowed for twenty years. I had always considered myself to be his last, true love.

"What new woman, dear?" I hissed.

Hux chuckled. "She's an old, I suppose one would say 'friend' from New York. She was in the theatre but has been retired for some time. You must meet her. I hear your tiny little hackles rising. If you are going to be difficult, put Bennett on the phone and I will speak to the management directly."

"That won't be necessary, Huxley. Bennett and I would be delighted to come to lunch. What color are the better bridesmaids wearing this season?"

"Try not to be an ass. See you Saturday."

Huxley's house is a big, yellow, three-storey clapboard colonial, built in 1799 by one of the Livingston daughters. The Livingstons, in case you have misplaced your early American history, received a 17th century land grant of some 160,000 acres and built glorious manor houses up and down the Hudson River. At some point this particular branch of the illustrious colonials spawned a midget whose picture Hux hung in an upstairs hall. It always reminds me of Jonathan Rauch's painting of Queen Victoria at the dwarf tossing trials.

Normally Huxley's luncheons are opportunities for the old guard and new folk to mingle, preen, and amuse each other in the warm bath of traditional manners and social mores. My first sense that Something Different was going on today was as we drove in: Medieval pennants bearing the English and French coats of arms fluttered on columns at the front of the house. A knight in full armor pranced around on a chestnut stallion in the middle of the circular driveway. Hoisting his lance, he made a pass at the gazebo, then turned sharply to trot toward our car, shouting, "Greetings! Forsooth! The bar's on the back porch!"

Bennett turned to me and said, "Are we simply underdressed or have Dutchess County and the fifteenth century suddenly collided in Huxley's front yard?"

"There's bound to be a simple explanation," I answered, clambering out of the car, "although I don't recall any mention of period costume. Perhaps it's a floor show? I hope this won't involve a cover charge."

I had anticipated something *intime* but it was a Rat Fuck, as we locals genteelly describe larger gatherings in the Valley. Bennett and I entered to find swarms of people wandering around the house, or standing in clutches, guzzling Bloody Marys or wine. Men in madras or seersucker jackets or vanilla gabardine suits gathered on the porch and in the living room, women in brightly colored slacks and silk blouses chattered with friends in

6

summery ensembles, all arrayed among Huxley's eclectic display of antiques and *objets*.

Mingling with the normally-attired were many young men and women wearing medieval dress---doublets, tights, and capes, and bearing all manner of weaponry---long bows and quivers of arrows, pikes, halberds, swords and shields.

Clutching my elbow as we looked around, rather slack-jawed, Bennett said, "Oh, I feel much better now. In the driveway I thought we were hallucinating. Now I see we've simply entered a time warp. Let's get a couple of meads and tonic."

I heard my name being crooned. "L-i-nnnnn-d-s-e-y!" and turned to see Huxley Smythe shuttling toward me in a pale lemon linen suit. Judging from the lapels, he must have worn it in college. Huxley is familiar to anyone who watched daytime dramas between 1952 and a few seasons ago. He wrote *Dark Again?*, *Suffer The Children*, and his last series, some said his best, *Winnetka*. He is the doyen of Hudson Valley society and our most outstanding purveyor of gossip, hearsay, scandal, and hard core news on who doeth what to whom.

"What in hell is going on here, Hux?" I asked between cheek pecks.

"I told you last year the moat needed some work, Huxley. Now look what's happened! The enemy is among us and eating your canapés!" Bennett laughed as he and Huxley shook hands.

"Didn't I mention that the cast of the Bard production of *Henry V* would be joining us for lunch?" Huxley raised his eyebrows in mock surprise. "Well, they have to eat like everybody else, especially the French ones since they'll all be dead in less than a week."

He continued, "This was all Francesca's idea of sales promotion. Whet everyone's appetite and boost attendance at the theatre. Mingle, darlings, mingle! Zounds and up your gauntlet!" Huxley stepped away to give instructions to Consuelo, his earnest but deeply lacking housekeeper, who was trundling toward the porch with four jars of salsa. "Not from the *jars*, dear! Dishes! Dishes! Silver, Consuelo! Cuença de plata!"

Eyeing the lads in tights and doublets, I asked Bennett, "I gather some are French and some are English. Which is which?"

Bennett slipped his arm around my waist and gestured to several young men having beers and playing with Huxley's pug on the porch steps overlooking the River.

"Those fellows in the simple, earthy-loden costumes are *English* foot soldiers. Their red belts and chevrons symbolize military strength and magnanimity. And those fellows over there," he gestured with his glass, "with heraldic motifs embroidered on their tunics---a recumbent stag, a repentant boar, a reclusive unicorn---those represent coats of arms of the thousand or so English lords who accompanied Henry into battle."

Then Bennett pointed across the room at a clutch of young men leaning on brightly painted shields, chatting with three women in what my mother would have called pedal-pushers.

"And those fancy pants are *French* lords. Noblemen were more tarted up beneath their armor, which," Bennett added in his best butlerese, "they are not wearing now as this is an informal luncheon. They wear the fleur-de-lis and have the blue and white emphasis---harlequin patterns, pales, bendlets, saltires, batons, and fesses."

"Saltires? Bendlets? Fesses? What is a fesse?" I asked, baffled.

"My darling, we haven't the time today to explore fully the language of heraldry. Permit me to spirit you away to one of my favorite crypts another time," he said with a mock leer. "Suffice it to say the designer has done her research and has provided us with an accurate, if perhaps too spotlessly clean, representation of what the English and French warriors wore for their fateful clash, on the fields of Agincourt, that St. Crispin's Day, 1415. Champagne?"

Flutes in hand, Bennett steered us over to a group of the swordsmen.

"What parts are you fellows playing?" asked Bennett.

"Unfortunately, I'm the Duke of York, one of the king's closest confidants---unlike these guys, who are mere yeomen"--- his two comrades in arms joined us and began a mock scuffle. "I fight valiantly. I direct a lot of the charge and I give a nice speech but, alas, I am felled by the French. I die beautifully."

"Don't I detect a bit of an accent??" asked Bennett.

The Englishman grinned and said, "My name's Brad Ruffin. I'm from Memphis originally, but my folks---they're right over there---live in Connecticut now. I'm a grad student in drama."

"And you must be a longbowman?" I said to another lad. "My!" I said, stroking his quiver, "what long arrows you have!" I think a little bawdy humor puts people right at ease, don't you? Are my Mrs. Robinson tendencies too close to the surface?

The boy nodded. "I said the same thing. I expected them to be the size we had at Scout camp but they're a lot bigger and so are the bows."

He unslung the longbow from around his chest. It was over six feet tall.

"These won the battle for the English. The French horses only had armor on their heads. A hail of arrows hit them in the backs and flanks and they went berserk! The French knights had to keep their heads down so as not to catch one in the face, couldn't even see where they were going. Hundreds of their foot soldiers died right away."

He gave a vee-sign. "This is how the English taunted the French. The French---who outnumbered the English by maybe ten to one---had sent word they would cut off the two bow fingers of every Englishman after the battle. The English made the vee-sign to show they were still in charge."

Bennett said, "Another story has it that the archers only held up the middle finger---and that's where we got *that* sign."

9

Clearly delighted by this nugget, the boys said, "Cool! And he *is* English. He should know!"

Brad turned and said, "Wait! I'd like to introduce you to my folks. Mom and Dad, meet Lindsey Brooks and Bennett Holcomb."

"Hello! I'm Dottie Ruffin and this is my husband, Louis."

The mother was whip thin and could have worn Fortuny with no problem. Her hair was honey blonde, impeccably cut. She must have been about fifty but looked to be thirtyish with no particular help except perhaps her eyes. Her husband had wavy chestnut hair, was also very fit in a blue seersucker suit with a blue polka dot bowtie, plus a gold signet ring on his left pinkie.

"That's a smart young man you've got there. He was just giving us some background on the history behind the play." Bennett has such beautiful manners.

Père Ruffin said, "Well, to me he looks like the poster boy for Sherwood Forest's fairies."

His wife laughed nervously. "Don't be silly, Louis. It's a period piece for heaven's sake." Turning to me she said, "Listen, Lindsey, I especially hoped I'd meet you today. Don Palmer and Jason have both mentioned you. We've been looking for a house around here. We're interested in three properties. I'd like to hire you to help us figure things out. The word is you have the inside track on lots of beautiful antiques, too."

My friend Kathy Hanover, who has just finished restoring a Stanford White house, and for whom restoration is a religion, strolled up and said, "I couldn't help overhearing. Which properties?"

"Yes, which properties? They're probably mine."

The voice was that of Geraldine Clinch ('I always clinch the deal'), realtor to the stars, as we call her in our part of the world, who swiveled into the group. "If you're planning on getting the Rensselaer estate, you'd best be prepared for a bidding war. Yesterday I showed it to Uma Thurman and tomorrow Bradley Cooper's looking at it. You should've signed with me."

"My goodness," said Mrs. Ruffin. "I had no idea the market was so busy up here."

"Oh, yes," said Huxley, reappearing with a plate of olives stuffed with gorgonzola. "Piranhas are swimming into our placid little pond. Oh, here's Mr. President."

Jason Priestly, the president of Bard, arrived and draped his arm around Dottie Ruffin's shoulder. "Oh, good, you've met. Lindsey is just the person to help you make up your mind on the house of your dreams. She's done my residence at the college. She's clever and she's fast."

"Terribly fast," intoned Bennett. Can't take him anywhere. Dreadful manners.

"Dottie, Louis, why don't you come for drinks and we'll talk about things," I invited. "Bring your sheets."

"I beg your pardon?" Dottie said.

"I mean, bring the spec sheets on the houses."

"Ah, yes."

Geraldine snapped, "You don't actually have a real estate license do you, Lindsey?"

"No, Geraldine, I don't. But I am licensed to carry a firearm and if you don't show a few more social graces to these out-of-towners, I might have to show it to you."

"Dear me," sighed the realtor to the stars.

I laughed. "Don't pay any attention to our wild talk. Southerners adore hyperbole. It's our way of livening up the conversation. How did Brad happen to choose Bard for graduate work?"

"He did his undergraduate work in New Haven, where Louis and I met, then came up here because he loved Bard's gorgeous new theatre and because the College mounts not only the classics but explores new works."

"And that's my job!" a man declared.

11

"Dr. Palmer!" boomed Jason, waving the fellow over. "The man of the hour!"

A tall man in a yellow tweed jacket and white trousers joined our circle. Palmer was a handsome man of about fifty, with expressive features and a mouth that made me feel he drank.

"Meet Donald Palmer. He runs our drama department and molds all these talented kids into the next generation of DeNiros and Streeps. He's directing all this historical mayhem."

"Don!" cried Dottie, giving him a sweet kiss and a hug. "How nice to see you!"

"Hello, Dottie," Palmer said, returning the cheek peck and grinning broadly.

"Louis, hello," he said, offering his hand. "How are you?"

"Good to see you, Don," replied Louis Ruffin, with a smile and firm handshake.

Dottie turned to me and said, "Don is Brad's faculty advisor. He's also directing him in *Henry V*."

Huxley joined us and bellowed, "Lindsey loves theatre! Tell her about what shows you've got in the works! She may even want to audition!"

Jason laughed heartily and said, "Now don't let Don tell you we're going to do Ionesco, we're not!"

Palmer faux-grimaced and said, "If Jason had his way, we'd be doing nothing but Noel Coward, Oscar Wilde, and Neil Simon! Keep it light, bouncy, and bright! Right, Jason?"

"The purpose of theatre *here* is to entertain, my dear boy," Jason answered. "Parents don't send us their aspiring thespians to be demoralized. They can be depressed by their history lectures. On stage, we want them to have some fun!" He slapped Palmer on the back again.

"We'd have a season of 'Paint your Wagon' followed by 'Barefoot in the Park' and 'Brigadoon' if it were left to Jason," Palmer continued, smiling. "Still, it's Jason who makes all this possible. He and our gracious underwriters." He half bowed with a sweeping salaam.

I said, "I don't think undergraduates have sufficient life experience to perform tragedies or the truly iconoclastic classics. I once saw my godchild in a college production of *The Balcony*. No one in the cast had the faintest idea of what Genet was talking about but they managed to emote and emote and emote for almost five hours. We nearly died."

Palmer laughed, nodding. "I agree. They can't yet fathom the heavy stuff. The main things we can give them are a sense of confidence, poise, and a certain amount of stagecraft--- which also means learning how to operate the sandbags and the scrims and shuffle scenery quickly and quietly. They're having a lot of fun with *Henry*---but the main thing they are learning is their way around a stage."

I said, "*Henry V* is one of the great plays. Always a favorite of mine."

"She invariably roots for the underdog," said Huxley.

Bennett said, "Oh, it isn't that. She's a closet Anglophile!"

"There's been a disturbing uptick in closet activity lately," said Huxley. "I myself am firmly in the closet."

"What closet is that, Hux?" asked Bennett.

"Why, the clothes closet! Is there any other kind?"

"Huxley," I said, "you do more for chartreuse than anyone since Dame Edna!"

"That's what my wife always said. We used to argue about who was the more flamboyant. But now! Look at all these young men! They're positively flashy! How can a simple soul like myself hope to turn the ladies' heads with such competition?"

Jason said, "Huxley, it's very kind of you to open your home to us today. Ticket sales should soar!"

"Yes, it's amazing what one can accomplish with a few well-placed bowls of salsa. I must away and see to those guests whom we wish to inveigle into season tickets."

Turning to the Ruffins, Jason said, "I hear you're buying a house up here?"

"Yes. Aside from Greenwich, we keep a little place in the city but my wife wants to be closer to the boy and I want to try some fly-fishing. There are more creeks around here than almost anywhere else until you get to Montana. We were just talking to Lindsey about helping us make up our minds."

Jason gave me a hug. "She's the girl to do it."

As the boys and the Ruffins returned to circulation, Huxley reappeared and said, "I rather like having shields and swords all over the house. I never met an escutcheon I didn't like. Oh, I don't believe you've met today's guest of honor?"

"That would be your old friend from New York? No, which is she?"

"Over there talking to Franklin." A woman stood with her feet planted wide apart, holding court with Franklin O'Connell and some of the cast, as well as several male civilians.

"That my dear is Cassandra Chappelle, the woman who originated the title role in *Harlot*.

"*Harlot*. The greatest American musical. Huh. That was what? Twenty years ago?"

"More like thirty-ish. I think she looks remarkable well. Of course, she's had some work done. Still, remarkably well," Huxley opined.

"Cassandra Chappelle," said Bennett. "I saw that production on a visit to New York. As I recall, her strip tease stopped the show. Have we heard of her since?"

"No," said Huxley. "She retired from the stage"---he made an extravagant gesture---"to devote herself to dear Baxter, a widower, and his four trusts. He was old enough to be her father---grandfather, really---but since she had never had either,

14

Baxter was her best shot. He lasted several years after they married and since his demise she has drowned her grief in world travel, perfecting her dissatisfaction with each day of life, and devoting herself to talking about her art. Cassandra has a tremendous talent for not painting, considerably more talent than when she does. She left New York for Santa Barbara and now doesn't paint out there, doesn't act, and worries the big bad forest fires will consume little Cassandra."

"How'd she wind up here?"

"A number of years ago she rented a house down the road for several weeks."

"How come I didn't meet her then?" I interjected.

"That must have been the summer you and Bennett were on an extended buying trip in France," Huxley answered. "But it hardly matters. Cassandra was not at her best. Like everything else in her life, the Hudson River Valley was *not enough* for Cassandra. Awfully *rural.* Absolutely *nothing to do.* No one ever *dresses for dinner.* Apparently in retrospect she's feeling a little kinder toward our brand of civilization. Franklin met her for lunch when he was in California buying yet another company. He suggested she come back for the Bard Festival---I believe 'triumphant return' was the way he positioned it---so here she is. Triumphally returned and annoying the hell out of Francesca by the looks of it."

My friend Francesca, Franklin's wife, a beautiful blonde, with a dazzling figure and a brain to match, stood beside a bower of wisteria, staring at the River across a glass of rosé and looking like she could bite the heads off babies.

Huxley took our elbows and steered me and Bennett over to Cassandra. She was a small woman, her hair in a blonde chignon, dressed in a long embroidered vest, almost like a page's doublet, over orange silk trousers.

"Cassandra, you must meet Lindsey Brooks. I can't think how your paths did not cross when you were here so briefly a few summers ago. And this is her portable blood donor, Bennett."

As we all shook hands, Bennett observed, "I believe I had the pleasure of seeing you in *Harlot!* You were magnificent." In their chatter that followed, the font of English unctiousness flowed so freely I expected him to kiss her hand.

At that moment we all turned as Francesca's voice carved a path through the air.

"Listen up, kiddies!" she barked. Francesca was wearing five shades of blue to bring out the sapphire in her eyes, which at that moment looked like lasers.

"Oh, dear," murmured Huxley. "Francesca has had quite enough of not being the center of attention. Where *did* I put my Richter scale?"

Swirling the long azure overblouse that flowed around her, Francesca strode over to Cassandra.

"Darling!" she exclaimed a little too loudly. "How can we thank you enough for dressing up our little afternoon with some *old* Broadway charm? Huxley, you have the most marvelous *old* friends! Cassandra, you must have so many reminiscences you'd like to share with us! Lunt! Fontanne! Barrymore!"

Cassandra laughed shrilly. "Darling, you are too funny! Lunt and Fontanne, indeed! Doubtless they were favorites of yours but they were a bit before *my* time! And you mustn't be so modest! How many people here know that Francesca was on the stage…*once*. What was that little thing, dear? *Moose Murders*, wasn't it?"

Moose Murders is widely regarded as the greatest egg ever laid on The Great White Way. This could be it, I thought, and murmured, "Huxley, you better move the majolica."

Huxley cleared his throat and interrupted, "Cassandra, someone wants to…" but Cassandra raised her voice a few notches and continued. "I can't remember now…were you in the chorus or just mounted on the wall in the title role?"

Bennett stepped into the breach manfully, positioning himself between the two women. "I say, Francesca! I can't recall your ever looking lovelier! That blue! Let me take you to the porch and demonstrate my fox trot!"

He took Francesca into his arms and whirled her toward the terrace as Artie Shaw played on Huxley's wood-burning turntable. As Francesca allowed herself to be hauled off the field of battle, Cassandra turned to us, laughed uproariously and said, "There's a worried woman!"

"Cassandra," Huxley replied, "I would appreciate it if you could be a bit more pleasant. Francesca is not the enemy. And no one wants a catfight!"

"Apparently she does! She started it." Cassandra lifted her glass, and finding it empty, headed for the bar.

"What the hell was all that about?" I asked.

"Wake up, Lindsey! You've seen Franklin this afternoon. He's hung around Cassandra like a teenager at the malt shop. Not a pretty picture for Francesca. But as for this last bit of fisticuffs…well, things may get worse."

"What about *Moose Murders?*" I asked. "Did you know about that?"

"Cassandra was being obnoxious. Francesca was not in *Moose Murders* or any other role. However, she cherished every young girl's dream of Becoming a Star. Somewhere between high school and the unhappy close of her third decade, Francesca tried her hand at the stage, at television specials, at commercials, at independent films, at modeling. Though she has as much pizzazz as the next blonde, an enormous personality, and, *God knows*, the tits to match, I suppose she didn't get the right breaks. Then she met Franklin and that, my dear, was her last and unquestionably most successful audition."

17

The next morning I found Bennett in the kitchen creating a fruit compote.

"Good morning, madame. I thought this morning, some yogurt and fruit and some of that gravel you like so much."

"Ah yes, the granola. Endorsed by the AMA *and* the highway department."

We carried our trays to the porch where breakfast takes place in the summer. The River floated lazily by as Catskill Creek glinted in the sunlight across the way. An eagle perched in a locust tree staring down. The water between the tides was still as glass. Pity the fish who chose to leap just then.

Biscuit rubbed against my leg.

"Sweetheart, you don't like cereal," I said. "Or yogurt or fruit. That's all we have to offer this morning."

"No, madame, that's not quite all." Bennett retrieved a baggie from his shirt pocket and emptied something into a little bowl sitting on his tray.

"And what is that?" I asked. "Little cat treats?"

"Yes, madame. Little bits of sautéed scallops left over from dinner last night."

"I ate my scallops, you ate yours. What was left over?"

"The one I prepared for Master Biscuit," Bennett said, leaning over to scratch the cat's ears as the little beast gobbled. Children in this hemisphere are starving and my cat is eating a diver scallop. Biscuit wandered into our yard last fall. He was so small we thought he was a kitten. Au contraire, a visit to the vet informed us: Biscuit was a year-old neutered male suffering from severe malnutrition. Apparently someone tired of him and dumped him on our dead-end road. After several months with us, Biscuit has doubled in length and breadth and now spends his days freeing the world of mice and chipmunks.

"What's on your docket today?" I inquired.

Bennett allowed he had a date for lunch in Hudson and was then heading over to Poet's Walk for some afternoon painting after the midday glare subsided.

"And you?" he asked.

"I'm lunching with Cassandra. Looking at her cottage."

"That was fast. A new client?"

"She's a woman who likes to get things done," I smiled.

I drove south down 9G watching mailbox numbers and turned up a steep drive climbing the limestone ridge that runs along the east side of the highway. As I rounded into the yard, I saw that the 'cottage' Cassandra had rented was a very substantial house. Vaguely Tudoresque-*cum*-Billy-Haines with a lot of cut stone and timbers, it was beautifully landscaped with extensive perennial beds, handsome shrubbery, and a long marble swimming pool on the southern end, its terrace punctuated with four Doric columns and a pergola. It had a superb view of the Catskills and just a smidge of river view from the north end of the property where I parked the little MG.

Cassandra came bounding down an iris-bordered stone path to meet me wearing a navy paint-speckled painter's smock, a pair of white Capri pants, and low beige espadrilles.

"Cassandra!" I cried, as we embraced, "what a marvelous spot! But it's hardly a cottage! It looks like Cary Grant---or should I say Rupert Everett? Or Rupert Graves?---might be lounging right on the terrace. Very golden age of Hollywood!"

"Isn't it a hoot?!" Cassandra giggled. "I rented it from a queen who needed cash for his art gallery. The place is on the market. If I get too involved in the re-doing, I might just buy it."

We joined arms and began to stroll around the property. "What sort of redoing are you thinking of?" I inquired, sensing a sizable commission.

"To start, just the basics and some desperately needed cosmetics in the main house. New furniture, fresh paint, get rid of the ghastly velour draperies."

Pointing east, she said, "See those buildings? The two barns? Those I want converted into French stables."

"*French* stables?" I laughed.

She giggled again. "My first priority? I want to redo the master bedroom *immediately*! Just between us girls, I have a friend nearby who has an overbearing wife. I want this to be a luxurious escape hatch for him. With me, of course!" she proclaimed gaily.

"I see."

Stepping close to me, she placed her hand on my arm and whispered, "If I confide in you, will you give me your word you won't betray me?"

I thought, 'Are you out of your mind? I hardly know you.' But aloud I said, "Definitely, darling! Tell me everything, I'm a crypt! Anyway, I probably don't even know the fellow."

"It's Franklin O'Connell. You find Franklin attractive, don't you?" she murmured, lowering her eyes.

I'm afraid my bulging eyes and dropped jaw betrayed me.

"Franklin?!?" I gasped. "You must be joking! Francesca never lets him out of her sight. And they seem"---I looked for the right words---"well, absolutely *devoted* to each other. They've been married thirty something years. They still hold hands in the movies, for heaven's sake."

Cassandra snorted.

"Holding hands! That's all he's interested in with her at this point. I'm the woman he needs---and wants---for this stage of his life." She continued. "He and I were lovers, many years ago, before he was in the Army. By the time he returned, I had moved on with my career and onto men who were *good* for my career. But I've always wanted him back. And I think I might just get him. After all, Francesca came from nowhere. And I am a Broadway legend!"

At the continued skepticism etched on my face, she shrugged, "Hell, it's worth a try! I'm a woman who keeps her options open, I'm a realist, not a fool! Plenty of fish in the sea. But Franklin! He'd be a great catch, wouldn't he?" She giggled again.

We sat on the terrace sipping a Rully before lunch was served. I had my notebook out making lists of furniture she wanted ("Mies! Noguchi! With just a splash of Chippendale!"), colors she liked ("White peaches---a Bellini by moonlight! Red crushed currants in the bath!") For someone who was supposed to be a painter, Cassandra had a very weird color sense---since when does one lacquer a foyer in aubergine? That went out with Studio 54.

Certain I couldn't hear one more word about gilded tie-backs, ebonized sconces, or trompe l'oeil niches by the pool, I changed the subject.

"Why'd you quit the theatre?"

"Because I knew I was never going to get a better role than my first big one when I was starting out. When you start at the top, kid, there's nowhere to go but downhill. Besides, for all the glamour, you have to crawl through a lot of filthy back rooms to get to the footlights. In my case, I had to put up with having the composer of *Harlot* fall in love with me."

"The composer? Louis Coen? He was one of the greatest talents ever."

"Oh, yes! You bet!" she grimaced and gulped some wine. "Tremendous talent and a tremendous sicko. That's the part the audience never sees. He'd bring home black hookers and make us get in bed together so he could watch. I was barely twenty, straight out of convent schools, and had barely been kissed.

21

Mother was the greatest stage mother of all time---kept me away from boys so they wouldn't interfere with her plans for me. Then I wound up being preyed upon by a satyr who pretended to be my mentor."

I shuddered. "How terrible! Must have been awful for you."

She nodded. "Yes, well, then I met Baxter and things straightened out. His grandfather was an early investor in Standard Oil and Ma Bell so he had bucks aplenty. We traveled the world, went every place I ever wanted to go. God bless him, he kept going until he was 94. Since he left everything to me, his two children hate me. They keep calling, can they come to see me, can they visit, shall we lunch. One damned thing after another.

"And, of course, there is never a shortage of suitors. Young, old, tall, short. They spring out of the woodwork no matter where I am. Here, New York, Florence, San Miguel, Montecito." She leaned toward me, "*But!!* How do I know it's me they're after and not my money! Ah, ha! That's the age-old question, ain't it? That's why Franklin is right for me. I don't need to worry he's after my millions when he's got billions of his own. By the way…" She thrust her hand into the smock's pocket and extracted an envelope.

"What do you make of this?" she asked.

It was a plain white number ten envelope with no return address. Inside, wrapped in a few sheets of typing paper was a first class ticket on a cruise leaving from NYC and headed to Shanghai. One-way.

"I'd say someone wants to get you on a slow boat to China."

◆ ◆ ◆ ◆ ◆

After our lunch, I trundled over to confer with Huxley.

We collected our coffees and sat on the porch to enjoy his view, the long southern aspect of the River.

22

"So she wants you to redo the house? Well, she has the money to afford you---if you can put up with her insane ideas. Her loft in New York looked like a cross between a Buddhist temple in Sri Lanka and a rehearsal hall in Finland. Everything was either brass or built-in. Dreadful. Why would she be spending serious money on a rental anyway?"

"She said she might just buy it." I decided not to spill Cassandra's beans about Franklin but simply said, "She says she plans to be around here for a while."

"What Cassandra says and what she actually does are often not remotely related. Still, it would be a nice job for you and your merry band of carpenters, plasterers, and upholsterers. After all, as you say so often---a girl's gotta eat."

The Moment for a Top Line on Your Heroine

That would be me, Lindsey Brooks.

I am Southern schooled. Afterward, I became an indentured servant at a big New York auction house. This lasted a few years by which time my ability to soak up facts and faces and master the finer points of several genres, to say nothing of my ability to hold my liquor (then, alas, more so than now) and charm birds and highly sought after estates out of trees got me noticed and got me a reputation as a comer.

I then left and started my own firm.

In London chasing a couple of early Bacons I'd heard about, I was having a martini at the Connaught. A man joined me at the bar and began chatting about antiques, then art, then invited me to join him for dinner. He proposed I help him and his agency---let's call it FBICIAMI5---examine a highboy they suspected of being a cache for microfilm.

The next morning we met in a warehouse off of Dunbar Street. I examined the highboy and found a tiny crevice behind a shard of marquetry where the dot was held. Another crevice held a SIM card. That bonus made him especially happy.

After that first assignment, and a nice fee for my troubles, I took other such jobs over the years. 'What sort of jobs?' you are probably wondering even though you are too polite to ask. Smugglers. Illicit goings-on at the intersection of espionage and eclectic furnishings. One thing and another.

My sort of expertise came in handy when the global shell games began including, dare I say relying on, not only stolen art work but artwork backed with stolen documents or decorative objects or furnishings stuffed with ill-gotten goods incriminating

Swiss bankers. I've seen missing Rembrandts behind declared Klimts. Once I could swear we were closing in on the Gardner heist but that one got away.

We also work for insurance companies recovering assets that have wandered away. Old maps can be very valuable and are extremely portable. One example: In our very own town of Hudson, a Bauhaus torchière, acquired by the seller at the Philadelphia Antiques Show, was re-sold to a man from Los Angeles after a bidding war at our esteemed local auction house, Stair Galleries. The buyer's interest in spending three times the $35,000 value of the lamp prompted a closer look. To everyone's amazement---save the buyer's, obviously---the lamp's bronze shaft housed a priceless, rolled-up, early 16th century Spanish map of California stolen some weeks prior from a Philadelphia antiquarian. The key to an overflowing Swiss bank safe deposit box once wound up inside the snout of an otherwise undistinguished Steiff bear. Amazing how these things work.

Smugglers are an imaginative and energetic subset of the larger criminal population. Citizens such as myself are happy to help the authorities bring them to justice. We do our part to keep your rates low.

These clients pay handsomely for my services.

After all, a girl's gotta eat.

Besides, I'm happy to help. Over time, I found I needed and enjoyed the excitement. Because *really*, how fascinating *can* one's fourteenth Rhode Island highboy be? I like finials as well as the next girl, but still.

Upon my return from London to New York, contract for two Bacons in hand, I got a call from an NYPD detective, Paul Whitbeck. He asked for help in a suspected stolen property case. A couple had so much stolen property---jewelry, silver, porcelain---the police assumed everything must be hot, including the art, but couldn't prove it.

Two of the paintings were by renowned Jamaican artists, Albert Huie and Judy MacMillan. By a coincidence, I had just visited Jamaica. While passing through Montego Bay, I had noticed "wanted" posters on telephone poles talking about stolen art. An old friend at Tryall told me several houses there had been burgled. Nothing taken except the art on the walls---stereos, cell phones, and laptops left untouched. Very odd. The trove Paul had cornered contained those purloined paintings, as well as a few others recently pilfered from a deodorant heiress in Cos Cob.

That coincidence established me as a star collaborator with the NYPD. To quote Paul Whitbeck, "Not only can she pull a rabbit out of a hat, the rabbit walks on water!"

Paul is now the sheriff of Columbia, the County just north of Dutchess. After his stellar career as head of detectives in midtown NYC, Paul retired early and came home to run his family's apple farm. Raising apples did not begin to use all of his brain and after he found his sons and their Jamaican crew were perfectly capable of managing the pruning, the upkeep, and the harvest with no help from him, Paul ran for sheriff. Shortly afterward, his wife died. Returning to law enforcement saved his life. When we reconnected over white corn at a farm stand, it was as though I'd reclaimed a long-lost brother (and one whose non-sequiturs are legendary). We have worked on a case or two up here.

But I digress. Crime detection is but a slender part of my portfolio. Far more of my time is spent on less turbulent tasks---selecting the right ecru for a foyer, supervising the arrangement of armorial porcelain, pacing and measuring twice to insure the perfect placement of upright yews to screen the Mercedes of the new owners of my latest rehab and flip.

Now that I have reached the shank of youth, I have largely left the madcap Manhattan art and antiques scene behind and repaired to the somnolent wilds of rural New York and my country house, the gaping maw, into which I have poured so many shekels and so much love.

Here, I dabble in real estate and cavort with the local worthies. I live in the country most of the time, keeping a minute pié à terre in town, and help out only occasionally with crime solving. Mostly I buy old houses, fluff them up, and sell them, or accept clients whose taste levels need a little upward nudging now and again.

To aid me in design projects and keep an eye on things at home, I lured an attractive English butler from his far too early retirement, plying him with a modest stipend and a cottage by the Hudson River. A widower, Bennett Holcomb wanted to move to America to be closer to his only son. He buttles for me and he paints landscapes for himself.

We both dodge questions about, as one woman put it, 'the nature of our relationship.' To save you the trouble of asking, I'll be upfront and say it's exactly what you would expect. When I related this inquiry to Bennett he laughed and said he got the same sorts of questions.

I asked, "What do *you* say?"

"Oh, madame. I say we are always completely upright."

PRE-THEATRE DINNER AT THE O'CONNELLS'

If you are a regular in Columbia or Dutchess counties, you know that Woods Road and then River Road are two of the most beautiful drives in the world, following the Hudson River past many of the great 18th and 19th century estates that caused the area to be known as America's Loire Valley. The former residents---Astors, Delanos, Livingstons, Vanderbilts, Millses, Philipses, and Roosevelts, among others---have been largely supplanted by 'celebrities,' as they are now known---actors, photographers, publishers, fashionistas, and pharmaceutical heirs, among a few state-and-friends-run historic sites. Gatehouses, entrance pillars, and miles of stone walls beyond which one can glimpse still stately allées (and closed-circuit cameras), remind us of an earlier grandeur now preserved by 21st century magnates and their money.

Franklin and Francesca O'Connell are two such examples of the American success story.

Both rose from rather humble backgrounds. Franklin has made many hundreds of millions, maybe even billions, by placing himself at the forefront of the green energy movement, both here and abroad; Francesca married him. Bright, charismatic, and gregarious, together they form the glittering center of social life in these parts. Franklin put together a vast wine cellar and Francesca put together a staff---'an entire village of Guatemalans,' as Huxley puts it, plus caterers and florists and decorators who transformed a fusty old Whitney mansion into a showplace.

Among their many good works, the O'Connells are big backers of Bard, the local college, and its musical festival and that

28

is why Bennett and I were headed down River Road now, for a gala dinner party celebrating the première of *Henry V*.

This particular evening, snug in Bennett's old 1954 Jaguar Mark VII saloon, our partner on the drive was Sheriff Paul Whitbeck, whom I had dragooned into joining us and who was on his maiden voyage to the O'Connell estate.

Paul is a man of simple tastes but unless he had been palling around with the Baron de Redé, not much would have prepared him for the O'Connells' lifestyle. Franklin and Francesca do their best to maintain the high standards set by earlier aristocrats and robber barons.

Franklin's money and Francesca's exquisite taste had restored the old estate to baronial splendor. The mile drive passed a few other houses on the property, any of which would have made city émigrés happy as larks. A complex of experimental solar and wind installations stood beyond stone barns, wherein Franklin houses his collection of vintage cars, and after a slight rise, a few hundred acres of lawn roll up to the house.

As we passed several families of deer, Paul muttered, "It's like a damn game preserve in here."

I smiled as he concluded, "You know, if I didn't love---I mean, really love, theatre, I might just change my mind about this."

We laughed. Paul loves theatre the way Bennett and I love mud wrestling.

Bennett handed over the Jag to Miguel Alvarado, who is married to the O'Connells' housekeeper, Rosa, the men got into their jackets, I reapplied lipstick, and we started up the stairs. In the reception hall we were greeted by attractive young men and women with trays of wine, cocktails, Champagne, and hors d'oeuvres so intricate and beautiful they might have been crafted in Fabergé's workshop.

The old Whitney mansion---Beaux Arts lines, exquisite moldings, rich paneling, marble and mosaic floors, twenty-five-foot ceilings, exquisite mahogany boiserie and painted panels, was a magnificent setting and was further augmented by the O'Connells' art collection.

Franklin had been stationed in England as an intelligence attaché during his Army stint. During his years there, he became intrigued by the work of British painters---the London school and others who revolutionized the art world, being on the cutting edge of the Pop Art movement, fantastic and mystic realism, and brutal art. He began his collection as a young man, buying on a soldier's pay, sometimes on a layaway plan, he once confessed. By the time his business had taken off and his fortunes were truly on the rise, there were still bargains to be had.

The Bacon head, probably George Dyer, in the main salon he got after the 1971 show at the Grand Palais for a fraction of what the work is going for now.

The Freud of Leigh Bowery, the flamboyant 1980s London performance artist, designer, and club fixture, a big canvas, perhaps 6 by 4 feet, hanging in the dining room, he found at a gallery in Soho.

The O'Connells' sitting room, tucked away on the second floor where on wintry evenings we sometimes had drinks à trois, held an homage to the artists of Bloomsbury. Franklin had located a superb Vanessa Bell painting of a nymph and satyr, a Duncan Grant portrait of Virginia Woolf, and a small portrait of Lytton Strachey by Dora Carrington.

A cerebral collection of young painters' work, reflecting Franklin's youthful awakening to art.

And, I have often wondered, perhaps because of the odds and ends he picked up in the intelligence community, had his time in England also awakened Franklin to the direction the energy markets would be moving in the later 20th century and into the 21st?

Amid the remarkable art and the intrinsic beauty of the old mansion, around 200 people in black tie mingled among the canapés and floated on a wave of general bonhomie.

"Hello, my dear!" a voice boomed and I turned to see Huxley looking resplendent in écru linen trousers, a violently plaid citron silk jacket, and black patent evening pumps sans socks.

"Thank heaven you're here," I purred. "I was so worried I might have to be pleasant to someone." Looking around, I observed, "What a great crowd! Hell of a lot of people I don't know."

"Yes, isn't it?" Huxley agreed. "Madame knows no bounds when it comes to soliciting support for the college. We all were told to bring at least one new person and I see you have enlisted your burly bodyguard for this evening's performance!" Hux remarked, smiling at Paul as they shook hands.

"Smythe! Haven't seen you since we ran you in for counterfeiting. Where's my fingerprint kit?" Paul retorted.

"Show me your weapon, sheriff!" Huxley crooned.

"Huxley, stop harassing Paul! We don't want any arrests to spoil this lovely evening!" Bennett smiled.

Having spent the twenty minute drive complaining about how he regretted exchanging his dress uniform for a rented tuxedo, how he wouldn't know anyone else at the party, and why was he hanging with the rich people anyway, Paul ran smack into the sheriff of Greene County, three town supervisors, and our state senator. Drinks in hand, they wandered off to confer on local politics.

An arm was thrown around my shoulder and I found myself staring into the compelling green eyes of Jason Priestly, Bard's president and chief pocket-picker. Jason is said to be an intellectual, and while it is not for the likes of me to opine on that, I do know he is a brilliant conversationalist, educator, and administrator, and can tell you that he excels at getting contributions to the college from all of us. I shiver when I see him coming; I dread another naming opportunity.

"Jason, darling!" I cried, giving him a big hug, and over his shoulder, "Bennett, hide the purse! The Artful Dodger is among us!"

"Hide mine, too!" Huxley chimed in, placing both hands over his breast pocket. He gestured to a waiter who passed a tray of glasses of rosé and Cosmopolitans.

"You people act like I'm being nice to you because I want something!" Jason burbled with mock horror, reaching for a glass. "I'm just feeling the love for Bard College tonight!"

At that moment Vernon Conroy, one of our most unctuous neighbors, oiled his way into our little group.

"What a jolly crowd tonight," he crooned. "Except for poor Francesca. She's seems miserable about something! Anybody know what?" he inquired with thick mock concern. Slipping his arm through Jason's, he purred, "Mr. President, I hear they're about to tap you to run the National Endowment. Put in a good word for me when the subject of your replacement at Bard comes up! Not that anyone could replace you..." He beamed at Jason.

"Lindsey," he continued. "You look stunning as usual."

"Good evening, Vernon," I replied. "How goes the life of the aging sycophant? And what makes you think Francesca isn't having a wonderful time?"

Vernon leaned toward Huxley. "Lindsey says Francesca isn't enjoying her own party. What say you, Smythe?" The man's a snake.

Huxley looked at me, then Vernon, then said, "Don't be absurd, Vernon. Francesca always likes it when she gets her money's worth---and we can all hear the coins clinking into the college coffers tonight!"

Trying to lighten the conversation, Huxley sang out, "Jason! What are you doing here? Shouldn't you be moving scenery for tonight's show or combing wigs or doing something productive?"

Jason laughed. Reaching his tuxedoed arm over a few feet, he snagged Don Palmer.

"*My presence* is not required at the theatre," Jason beamed, "because our own impresario has the job well in hand!"

Palmer, elegant in a white dinner jacket, shook hands with all of us and said, "Bask in my presence while you can, chums, because I'm just here for drinks." He consulted his watch. "In precisely three minutes, I exit this scene and pop over to the theatre for last minute madness and nerves. Jason, do you have prepared remarks for the evening's finale? Or will you ad lib?"

"My inspiring words are being typed even as we speak. My secretary will deliver them to you backstage very shortly. We're excited to see the show, Don! Break a leg!"

"Well, then, I'm off to the stage!" Palmer cried. "See you on St. Crispin's Day!"

At that moment, our hostess swept into the room. Francesca came directly over, planted a kiss on my own and the other assembled cheeks and sang out, "Isn't this a great party! Do you know I have already met ten people I'd never heard of and sold them season tickets to the fall program!"

Huxley boomed, "Selling tickets! My dear, is there no task too small? And I suppose you made each and every one of these canapés in your spare time?"

Francesca laughed, "You know I love to cook! I made all these canapés and everything else you'll be wolfing down tonight! I also stitched up this little old thing!" Francesca twirled in a jade green, beaded cocktail number that screamed Bergdorf and must have cost $15,000 if it cost a dime.

"You're the perfect little homemaker!" I cried, getting into the act and giggling. I love a fun hostess and I love getting the Coveted Best Guest Award. Francesca gave my arm a little squeeze. "I've got to show you something. Will you gentlemen excuse us while Lindsey and I have a little girl talk?"

Scooting out the back door, we began a leisurely stroll down toward the pool house, a lovely little glass and bluestone post-modern structure.

Eyeing the herbaceous borders, I asked, "Francesca, do you have a new gardener? I notice a lot of new plantings," and indeed the borders along the walk had come a long way. For many years, since the O'Connells had bought the house, the flower beds had been the stepchildren of the grounds crew and consisted of clashing annuals in carpet bedding, no less. Grim. I have never been a big fan of yellow and orange Lantana or pink Dianthus but hundreds of each had constituted the entirety of the plantings, at least until this year when the White Flower Farm Fairy had apparently flown in.

Francesca laughed. "The flowers were laughable, weren't they? I've grown up. Last year we went to Sissinghurst and Hidcote and a couple of other English manor houses and the plantings took my breath away. I realized then that I needed to give more direction. So I got a list of what Sackville-West had planted and bought a couple of Penelope Hobhouse books and gave directions to have their borders duplicated. One can't leave everything to the help. I also bought the biggest plants I could get my hands on and had the soil in the borders completely replaced. I had no idea how much dirt could cost but this is the best money can buy."

Not for Francesca the enrichment over time with compost and hand-spading of fecund matter. She simply put her checkbook where other people put their vegetable peelings.

"Well, it looks marvelous!" I said. "Where did you get peonies this size? And the iris! Absolutely magnificent."

Smiling brightly as she returned the waves of a group back on the terrace, Francesca continued, "Last fall, my sister called me about an auction at yet another Long Island estate being torn down. There were a lot of furnishings she thought we could use. The grounds were also gorgeous, so I asked the people handling the estate sale what their plans were for the gardens. Well! They planned to *asphalt* the entire place around the co-ops they were building so I sent Big Ben out with his people and a couple of backhoes. We dug the entire place up lock, stock, and bareroot and put them in the greenhouses over the winter. Then this spring we put them in the borders. It worked out well, wouldn't you say?"

"Brilliantly!"

When we rounded a giant clump of rhododendrons and were out of sight of the house, Francesca abruptly stopped and grabbed my shoulder roughly.

"Listen up, Lindsey! I didn't get you out here to talk about these god-damned flowers! I want you to tell that slut to stay the hell away from my husband."

"Who are we talking about?" I asked, the epitome of innocence.

"You know damned well who I mean. That bitch Cassandra. What do you know about her?"

"I met her for the first time at Huxley's last week, when knighthood was in flower."

Francesca went on angrily. "She's all over Franklin like a cheap suit! And when I'm standing right there! She couldn't be more obvious if she were a flashing neon sign saying, 'Lay me! Lay me!' " Sometimes Francesca's distant upbringing surfaces when one least expects it.

I shook my head. "Oh, come on, Francesca! She's a professional flirt! Half the people here probably think she wants to get in their pants. I thought she even looked at me in, well, a winsome sort of way...." I smiled.

"This is not funny and I'm not putting up with it."

"Well, Francesca, surely you've met flirts before? And for that matter, I flirt madly with Franklin. You have a very attractive husband."

"That's my point. He's *my* husband! *Your* flirting is just friendly affection. *Hers* is a *hell* of a lot more than that. I don't like it---*and I don't like her.* Do everybody a favor. Tell her if she knows what's good for her, she'll back off."

◆◆◆◆◆

When we returned to the house, Francesca went into the kitchen and I found Bennett and Huxley admiring a new sculpture on a plinth in the north parlor. Then we all watched Franklin waltzing Cassandra through the glittering throngs.

"Cassandra certainly seems to be enjoying herself," I remarked, slowly regaining my composure after Francesca's tirade.

"As well she might, being the O'Connells' guest of honor tonight," Huxley replied.

"What!? Why, pray, is she the evening's honoree?" I inquired.

Huxley said, "I thought you knew. Cassandra has agreed to underwrite *Henry V.*"

◆◆◆◆◆

Bennett, Hux, and I continued sipping, observing Franklin maneuver Cassandra among the guests, introducing her to one and all, his palm rarely leaving the small of her back. Francesca stood seething at the opposite end of the terrace surrounded by a clutch of lady friends, all glowering.

Bennett said to Huxley, "Tell me about Franklin."

"Franklin's father came over on the boat in the Twenties, managed to keep his family together through the depression as a cobbler, then after the economy straightened out, began making bespoke shoes for Wall Street types. Out of college, Franklin went to Officers Candidate School, served in the Army for a few years, got his degree, then joined a Wall Street firm as an energy analyst, distinguished himself, began his own consulting firm, and shortly was spearheading the green energy movement. He backed some people with new lighting patents, went to Holland

and Belgium to see new technologies, and got into wave power before anyone else. He then went to Bolivia and bought about 20 years worth of lithium futures, went to Canada and invested in vanadium, got some investors and started mining lanthalum and promethium. Don't even ask me what all those things are, I learned all of this from flash cards," Huxley said, rolling his eyes.

"They're rare earths," said a voice behind my back and Brad Ruffin's father, Louis, joined us. "Before I decided on architecture, I worked one summer for a geology company out west. The field gets more interesting every day. Electromagnetics is so hot just now, pardon the pun. That is the only fuel source that makes sense for so many applications, to say nothing of the importance of rare earths in developing improved capacities in batteries. Franklin is a clever man. Ah, here's my beautiful wife," he said, and Dottie Ruffin joined us, svelte and lovely in a taupe silk cocktail sheath, slipping her arm into her husband's.

"Do these people always entertain on this scale?" she asked, smiling. "What an evening! But, if you'll excuse us, I'm going to drag Louis over to say hello to our hosts," and the Ruffins moved away.

"Where were we?" Huxley asked.

"You were telling us about the O'Connells," Bennett answered. "You just covered Franklin. What about Francesca?"

Huxley made a little moue and answered, "That's a rather different story. Francesca was a sales rep calling on his firm selling some sort of filaments, or early diodes, or lasers, is the way I heard the story."

I said, "I was not aware she had a science background?"

"Who said anything about science?" Huxley snorted. "Francesca hardly needed to know one end of a diode from the other---no, no, no! *Not* when she was possessed of a sparkling personality, *and* a well-developed other 'Per-son-al-i-ty' as the old song has it. Plus, she had a strong spirit of upward mobility sadly lacking in Franklin's first wife.

"Francesca came from some backward hollow in Pennsylvania. Escaping her roots, she has become the embodiment of ambition and civic fervor. Obviously she's quite beautiful and a truly extraordinary clothes horse. There's a plaque honoring her at the entrance to Bergdorf's. But as she says, when Franklin pretends to grumble about her conspicuous consumption, 'As long as you keep making it faster than I can spend it, I don't see a problem.' "

Back inside, I thought about Francesca's unease. I thought about the slow boat to China. Then I busied myself sampling the canapés which were scrumptious.

Round dining tables were arranged throughout the ballroom with beautiful settings, as usual. Tall centerpieces featured pale blue iris, dark blue Monk's Hood, violet acanthus, and trailing ivy. Lilac napkins with slightly darker lilac tablecloths lay atop white damask. The place cards found me at Franklin's table just a few seats away from Cassandra. Jason was on Cassandra's right.

The salads had been preset.

As the staff circulated pouring wine, Jason turned to me and said, "I've been meaning to talk to you about helping us pull together an Alumni Suite. Quite a few fine pieces of furniture and porcelain have been left to the college over the years. Make a nice place for alums to have a cup of tea, maybe some wine, meet each other. Does that sound interesting?"

"Yes," I said, thinking it sounded like a tax deduction. "What sorts of things do you have?"

But at that moment his phone rang.

Pulling it out of his pocket, he said, "Palmer, old boy! You're in the wings? Everything under control? Yes….yes…good. Notes on the lectern in the wings. Got it. See you soon. Ta-ta. Now, Lindsey, let me tell you about some of the furniture we've inherited."

Our conversation continued as waiters began to serve dinner.

As chocolates and petit fours were being passed around at the end of the delicious meal, Franklin stood.

"I'd like to make a few remarks. Everyone knows the battle of Agincourt---fought in 1415, some twenty-five miles south of Calais, where a few thousand Englishmen defeated ten times their number of French knights. There are a lot of analogies I could make tonight, but I'm going to limit myself to fifteen."

Everyone groaned but Franklin waved his hands, saying, "Relax! Just kidding! I'm only going to do three.

"First, let's talk about small colleges. We may not be Harvard but Bard has been acclaimed as the best in small colleges for the third year in a row." He paused for applause. "Next, let's consider our theatre. We may not be the biggest, we may not be the Met, but we are staging the fifth original production in as many years, all of which have gone on to play at important festivals around the world." He paused for more applause.

"And finally, we have a new patron, and she's not very big either. She's about five foot two and, yes, her eyes are blue." I began to shift nervously in my chair and I noticed others doing the same; Franklin was on thin ice here.

"Yes, she may be petite but she is a giant patron of the arts. May I present our evening's honoree and the underwriter for our new production of *Henry V*, Miss Cassandra Chappelle. Let's all stand for a toast."

As bade, we all stood. Francesca was the last to rise from her seat.

Cassandra raised her glass, acknowledging the applause.

Looking out over the crowd, she said, "I can't tell you how happy I am to be a part of the wonderful work that is being done here at Bard. I feel I'm finally home at last."

Francesca slammed her napkin down and swept from the room.

CURTAIN GOING UP!

After dinner came the great exodus. Cars were brought around by the village of Guatemalans and we all hied off to the theatre, an eight-minute drive away.

Cassandra came over and asked, "Have you got an extra seat for me?" Paul and I put her up front with Bennett.

Bard's theatre is a brilliant Frank Gehry design capped by a gleaming, undulating steel roof. The architect has said the front façade of the building may be interpreted as a theatrical mask, its abstract form preparing visitors to be receptive to the variety of performances staged within the several venues inside the theatre.

Opened in 2003, the building's $62 million construction was largely underwritten by Richard Fisher, a Baker scholar at the Harvard Business School and a former chair of Morgan Stanley. There are three performance spaces; tonight's was staged in the largest, the handsome Sosnoff Theatre, an acoustic delight swathed in honey-colored fir veneer and seating about 900 before a generous proscenium and an orchestra pit. In an especially sweet touch, the theatre's seats are upholstered in fabric woven with the names of Bard's 2003 graduating class. Martin Sosnoff, who paid for the theatre, runs an investment fund; he and his wife, Toni, partnered with Fisher and Gehry to create a world-class theatrical venue.

The theatre blazed with lights as several hundred people streamed across the campus toward it and filed slowly in. We joined the throng and took our seats in the block Francesca had reserved in the main theatre.

Cassandra entered as though she were making her debut at Covent Garden. She whirled her stole, engaged in animated conversation with several couples on the aisle, waved gaily to friends across the hall, embraced those seated in front and behind her, and finally blew a kiss to Franklin who sat a few rows away with Francesca.

The house lights dimmed. As the curtain rose to reveal a backdrop of giant English and French coats of arms against the field of battle, a trumpet fanfare rang out from the back of the house. King Henry's army began marching down both aisles with the king's battle standards flying amid drummers and bagpipes. Hit by a spotlight, Henry ran up to the lip of the stage and delivered his first speech.

Paul sat transfixed. He who had grumbled about tonight looked like a little boy at the circus. Theatre is a wonderful thing and regional theatre is often the very best.

Shortly, as the battle commenced, warriors began to fill the stage. Clever use of rear projection showed a cloud of French nobles arriving on horseback. Their numbers grew until they were many times the size of the English troop. Multiple lasers criss-crossed the stage as torches flashed, swords and shields clashed, and the roar of battle grew.

English longbowmen let fly many actual arrows---how realistic, we all gasped---and the French began to fall. Their knights, gotten up in man-*cum*-horse costumes, foundered. Unable to advance, the French were pulled from their mounts, dashed against the stage, and slain with broadswords. The spectacle was marvelous.

At the battle's end, the curtain rang down, and the audience cheered wildly. We were still applauding when the curtain was pulled violently apart and an actor in doublets cried, "We need a doctor! Is there a doctor in the house?!" A man leaped from the audience, ran to the stage, and disappeared behind the curtain. Moments later, a security guard came and asked Paul to come backstage. Paul grabbed my hand and pulled me up with him.

"Why me?" I protested as we ran toward the stairs.

"Because you know your way around this place."

Pressing our way behind the curtain and through actors and stagehands, we found an English nobleman lying with an arrow embedded in his tunic, the doctor kneeling over him. Several other soldiers stood by with similar arrows also bristling from their chests.

The doctor stopped his examination and looked up at us.

"He's dead."

The president of the College stood a few feet away. Jason gasped and looked as though he had been stabbed.

"That's impossible!" He turned to Palmer, the director, who was kneeling beside the boy---I now realized it was Brad Ruffin---and said, "You're in charge! What the hell has happened?" and to Paul, "What do we do now?"

Paul stood up and said sharply to Palmer and Jason,

"No one leaves this stage."

Seizing Palmer by the shoulder, he ordered, "Get your security people to lock these doors now! Keep the cast and crew right here until we get some officers in place. Lindsey, get rid of the audience."

I nodded at Paul, then took Jason's arm, pulled him aside, and said, "Jason, you have to go out front. Calm the audience. Say the production has been halted because of a medical emergency. Do not say that anyone is dead. Ask the people to hold onto their tickets. Tell them the play will be restaged at a later time. Thank them for coming and tell them to go home."

Leaving Paul barking calls for an ambulance and officers into his cell phone, I asked to have the house lights brought up, and propelled Jason through the curtains. The audience listened as Jason, shaking slightly, made his announcement. I returned to my seat to get Bennett to join me backstage to help Paul in the commotion. Franklin and Francesca leaned over to me and Franklin said, "What's going on? What's the trouble?"

43

Before I could answer, Cassandra abruptly stood up, threw her arms wide, and moaned loudly.

She cried out, "What is happening? Help me! Help me!"

She swayed unsteadily, then gathered her stole about her and began to pull at it. She thrust one arm straight up while grasping her throat with her other hand.

From a few rows back, Franklin leaned forward. "Cassandra?" he called.

Cassandra shrieked again and crumpled backward. Bennett leaped to catch her as she sank into the aisle.

She shook violently, then lay still. Bennett placed his fingers against her neck.

"I'll get the doctor!" I whispered.

"No need, Lindsey," Bennett answered, holding her. "She's dead."

A COMPLICATION

The morning after the opera, Paul called early as I was on the porch watering plants.

"Lindsey, I have some bad news, some good news, and some better news. Which do you want first?"

Sinking into a chair and throwing my legs over the arm, I answered, "After last night, good would be better but let's have the bad first."

Paul began, "Did you notice that Hank Hill, the Dutchess County sheriff was not on the scene last night?"

"You know, I really did not. I'm not at all sure I even know Sheriff Hill. Why was he a no show? Out of town? Gone fishing? Whatever, a hell of a lot of his deputies appeared pretty damned instantaneously, didn't they?"

"Yes, that's so," Paul nodded. "Fast response from a well-trained group of young officers. Hank runs a tight ship. Hank was missing in action last night because he's been laid low. Two discs in his back no longer want to play nicely with the other discs and are pushing his spinal cord around."

"Yike!" I said, wincing. "Back trouble is awful! The poor man. He needs to take care of that right away."

I paused. "That is the bad news?"

"That's the bad news."

"And the good news?"

"The good news is that I had coffee at Hank's house this morning with a few of his best men. They were unanimous in supporting Hank's request that I step in and handle this case while Hank is out. He's scheduled for surgery tomorrow."

I saw where this was going. "What about the well-trained young deputies?" I asked.

"That's the thing, my dear girl. They are young. I trained Hank myself. He's building a first-rate department but none of his officers has ever participated in, much less led, a suspicious death investigation. I've agreed to run it until Hank is back. We'll have the department's capable assistance, of course."

"We who is going to have their capable assistance?"

"That's the better news---you and I are going to work this case together! It'll be like old times!"

"What old times? Years ago we did some art heists, a smidge of smuggling, and, OK, that one murder at Olana, but..."

Paul interrupted, his voice rising. "*Which* you were quite instrumental in solving, let's not forget! Credit where credit is due, my dear!" Paul sounded so happy. Was *I* happy? Did I want this?

"I don't know. I've got a couple of new clients."

"Well, you're down one new client, dear. She just popped. Oh, come on, Lindsey. Truth, justice, and the American Way need your help! It'll just be until Hank's back. And get a move on, dear! We're due at Jason Priestly's office in an hour."

He slammed down the phone. I slammed down my watering can and went to find some clothes. I found Bennett in my dressing room laying out a navy jacket, chinos, and a frilly silk print blouse.

"Since when do you work wardrobe?" I asked.

"Getting you ready to meet the Sheriff, madame. When the phone rang, I was in the kitchen and saw his name on the caller ID. A child of four could have deduced that he was inveigling you to participate in this murder investigation. Am I correct?"

"Yes, Bennett, you are correct, though I don't recall clairvoyance on your resumé," I snapped.

"Now, now, madame. We know you like a good case. Do it for St. Crispin."

THE YOUNG NOBLEMAN'S DEATH

The land that is now the Bard College campus dates back to a vast tract bought from the Indians in 1680 by Colonel Peter Van Rijn. A village grew up to support the eventual manor house with all the usual appurtenances of that era; grist mills, a lumber yard, housing for servants, merchants and tap houses for the local residents, and meandering cattle paths throughout the several hundred acres.

The grounds began their metamorphosis into a carefully landscaped estate in the 1830s, when Robert Donaldson of North Carolina acquired the property and gave it the name Blithewood. He commissioned Andrew Jackson Downing, one of the foremost landscape artists of the day, to design the grounds. In 1853 Blithewood was purchased by John Bard of Hyde Park, who in 1860 gave a corner of the estate for the founding of St. Stephen's, a college to preserve the tenets of liberal education for young gentlemen when most were being trained to go to war. Many students later entered the Episcopal seminary in New York.

St. Stephen's became Bard College in 1928, the same year it became an undergraduate college of Columbia University. The faculty was strengthened and enriched in the 1940s by the addition of many distinguished émigrés from Europe. Over the years, Bard faculty has included numerous MacArthur honorees as well as Nobel and Pulitzer Prize winners.

As the college grew in enrollment and stature, the many clapboard houses, stone mills, and workers' barracks scattered throughout the little hamlet of Annandale-on-Hudson were assimilated and joined by classrooms, residence halls, libraries, art studios, administrative and faculty offices in a variety of architectural styles. Tudor revival, Italianate, Jacobethan, Queen Anne, Victorian, Bauhaus, modern and post-modern creations now dot the campus. Its bucolic setting---a great deal of the campus is wooded, criss-crossed by unpaved trails that were once those cow paths---gives the campus a feeling of tranquility. It is an idyllic place for students to learn and for faculty to teach. Its academics are nationally recognized. Bard maintains campuses in New York City, Boston, California, Germany, and Russia, bringing Bard's mission to the world. In settings urban and rural, from programs at small institutes to large universities, the college has extended its global reach from the hamlet of Annandale to the wider world.

I parked in front of the President's office, pulling in beside Paul's car.

"Morning, Miss Brooks," the sheriff said, waving me over. "Please join me for a moment in my cruiser."

I got in and said, "You know, I have a number of things to do today. Why do you need me for a---what did you call it? A 'suspicious death'? What's suspicious about it?"

"Why don't you tell me what you saw---and what you think happened."

"There was a fight scene with arrows flying around. One hit the boy, poor Brad Ruffin, in the chest. If that didn't kill him, and that would have been an accident, I figured he had an aneurism. Or a stroke. Both are rare in a twenty-something but it happens."

Paul sat quietly.

I pursed my lips. "I gather you know more?"

"It's bad, Lindsey. The body went to the medical examiner last night." Paul shook his head. "He wasn't killed by the arrow stuck through the Styrofoam on his chest, not by an aneurism or stroke. Somebody stuck a knife in him. Stuck it in six inches between the third and fourth ribs. Punctured a lung and a ventricle."

"Jesus," I said. "It's murder."

Paul and I walked up the steps to see the president of the college.

A scholar who had combined the study of archaeology, B.S. Harvard, with a Masters in Greats at Oxford, Jason Priestly had arrived at Bard some twenty years before. His infectious enthusiasm for finding and promoting the scholar and the love of learning in everyone he met---students, professors, and, perhaps most propitiously, wealthy alumnae and parents, had accelerated the growth of the college, propelling significant expansion on all fronts---curriculum, faculty, drama, music, buildings, and those educational outposts in other towns.

Jason personally leads archaeological expeditions not only into the Adirondacks, where he points out mastodon teeth in the streams as students wade, but throughout New England, surveying the dolmens of Phoenician outposts in New Hampshire, petroglyphs in Connecticut, and stone altars in Massachusetts. Beyond his home territory, Jason has led students to the sites of ancient Troy and Delphi, where surveys of ruined temples are combined with the study of the Oracles and Homer's poetry.

As Paul and I were escorted into his office, Jason was on the telephone but stood to greet us, motioning us to seats in front of his desk, a large mahogany oval, scattered with a variety of mementoes---gold weights, a statue of a minotaur, and a replica of a bust of Pericles. At least I think it was a replica. What looked like a dinosaur vertebra topped with a thick plate of glass sat among some chairs and settees, functioning as a coffee table.

Jason is a tall man with abundant, wavy, gray-flecked blonde hair and green eyes framed by tortoise-shell glasses. He carries himself like an athlete and radiates energy. It suddenly occurred to me that he might be modeling his personal style on Patrick Fermoy. His graduate years at Oxford had left him with a faint English accent and a trace of English mannerisms.

49

Continuing his animated telephone conversation with what I gathered was a foundation considering a grant proposal, Jason strode around the office, adjusting books on shelves, punctuating his conversation with extravagant gestures, now and again throwing a wink our way---we, his other audience---consulting his desk calendar, then jotting something, darting over to thrust that note out of his office door, and finally ringing off with a flourish and a clap of his hands. The conversation concluded, Jason whipped off his suit jacket to reveal braces woven with some insignia, probably that of his Oxford college.

"Come!" he sang out, bounding around the desk to shake hands. "Thank you so much for your patience. One never knows when a foundation will reach out---but it goes without saying that one is duty-bound to take the call!" He laughed in the hearty way of exuberant professors.

"Let's sit over here." He moved us to a sunny conversation grouping of two couches, four wing chairs, and that dinosaur vertebra. He glanced at his watch. "It's a lucky thing you caught me this morning. In almost no time I'm heading over to Massachusetts---leading a group of sophomores and juniors to study the stone beehives of the Upton Chambers. Do you know that place just outside of Boston? Marvelous!

"Marion!" he called, and a young brunette walked briskly in with a tray of coffee. "This is a terrible thing, terrible," Jason said, shaking his head sadly, as he poured cups for Paul and me. "Young man drops dead. Who'd believe it? Could have happened to any of us! Carpe diem et cetera, what!?"

After our coffees were in hand, Paul cleared his throat and opened his mouth but Jason continued without a pause.

"Needless to say, I was concerned about the College's potentially adverse position on this but I've spoken to the boy's parents this morning. They are beyond distraught, naturally! But they realize this needs to be handled in a civilized manner and brought to a dignified conclusion with as little sensationalism and invasion of privacy as possible."

"You mean we need to solve the murder," Paul said.

"Murder!" Jason snapped. "What on earth are you talking about? This was a heart-breaking, freakish accident! An arrow that tragically punctured a young man's heart! Not a murder!"

I answered, "I'm afraid not, Jason."

Paul shook his head.

"Dr. Priestly, the boy's body went to the medical examiner last night. He wasn't killed by the arrow stuck in his chest"---and glancing at me---"and not by an aneurism or a seizure. He was killed by a knife stuck six inches in. Death would have been damned quick. Of course, this occurred in the middle of a battle scene with so much going on it is understandable nobody noticed that one of the people flailing around on the ground was truly injured. Except the killer, of course. In all probability, he also shoved the arrow into the boy's chest and maybe hoped we wouldn't get around to finding the other wound. He wanted it to look like an accident. The problem was that the sternum blocked the arrow. The kid would have been sore but he would have been a long way from dead."

Jason's face had paled. "I can't believe this. This can't be happening. Not here! This is a respected college, not some sort of back alley!"

Paul paced around the office as he continued.

"Obviously he was killed by someone who was on the stage at the same time he was. Which means it was either someone in the cast or crew. We're going to be talking to the entire lot, but I want to start with the director after seeing you. What was his name again?"

"Palmer," Jason said hoarsely. "Donald Palmer."

"Where's his office?"

"Just across the campus green. In the Tudor building."

51

"While we walk over to his office, I want you to call him. I want a list of everyone in the cast and crew, their addresses and phone numbers. I also want your office to contact these people immediately and tell them to stay around as we'll need interviews with everybody. And I think it might be wise for you to stay around, as well."

Jason sat in stunned silence for a moment. Then he said, "Of course."

"I'd also like to set up an office here on campus, make it the base of our operations. It will save a lot of time."

Jason answered, "One of the houses down on Ludlow is vacant. We just relocated the faculty who used it. It has wireless, copiers, desks, everything you should need. Do you want to see the boy's parents?"

"Of course," I said "We were with them last night at the O'Connells' dinner. They must be devastated. Where are they staying?"

Jason nodded. "They're at the Madalin Hotel in Tivoli. I broke the news to them last night."

Paul said, "Please call them. Ask if we can meet at their hotel at noon. Now I want to talk to Palmer."

"I've already called him. I thought you'd want to see him just as a matter of procedure---now I see it is a great deal more serious than that. He's in his office and he's expecting you."

"And another thing," Paul said. "Don't repeat anything of what I've told you this morning. Not one word."

We walked across the tree-lined commons toward the great pile that housed the drama department.

"What about Cassandra?" I asked.

"She's at the funeral home in Rhinebeck," Paul said. "One of you is going to have to make some arrangements, I suppose."

"No, I mean what about her autopsy?"

Paul frowned. "Why do we need an autopsy? She keeled over. She probably had a heart attack."

"You don't find it mildly odd that we witnessed two deaths within a few moments of each other? I'm not saying there *is* a connection, not saying it is more than a weird coincidence, but I think I would check it out."

"An autopsy is going to take a next of kin or an inquest."

"Can't you just order it?"

"I could, but the press would be a little weird."

"How would they become aware of it?"

"You don't know much about funeral directors, do you?"

"Why put a lid on it? Two deaths just too much for one small college to manage?"

Paul snapped, "Lindsey, you are not interrogating me! We are both going to interrogate Palmer! We can discuss what, if anything, needs to be done about Cassandra Chappelle at some point, but please! Knock it off for now."

As we approached the Drama building, two of Paul's deputies pulled alongside us in a cruiser. They hopped out.

"Sheriff, we got your call."

"Get every man we have over here. I want every inch of that stage, that entire theatre searched for any sort of knife, letter opener, screwdriver, knitting needle, any damned pointed thing that could have been the weapon that night. I want every bush looked at, every blade of grass moved, every chair picked up, every desk, closet, toilet, and cabinet gone through. I want the scenery, the costumes, the props---anything that is in that building, I want it gone over. I want that weapon found. Clear?"

"Yes, sir." And they moved away quickly.

Drama in the Drama Department

As we stepped inside the building, the summer glare was swallowed by walls and floors of dark walnut, the fragrance of mowed grass and roses replaced by the musky verbena of a hundred years of waxing. We walked up a wide staircase to the second floor and knocked on the door marked, 'Donald Palmer. Chair, Drama Department.'

At our knock, the door was thrown open with a flourish.

"Please come in. God, this is awful, isn't it?"

Palmer admitted us into a large room that looked as much stage set as office. Hamlet's skull sat atop a bookcase. Heavily fringed burgundy draperies were drawn back to frame an alcove and a window seat. The niche was lined with photographs of various actors on stage, Playbills, and dried boutonnières. Capes, wigs, plumed hats, and various swords, daggers, and halberds were arrayed on the walls. Dark wainscoting went halfway up the walls and above the wood, framed theatre posters hung against faded ochre walls. A large round table was piled with scripts, books, and masks. The director was a big man, certainly six feet four or so, very trim in a black linen jacket over chinos. As Paul and I took seats in front of his desk, Palmer ran his hands through his hair repeatedly, shook his head, and finally leaned forward, hands cradling his forehead. He began to cry, then quickly pulled out a handkerchief and, turning away from us, dried his eyes, and composed himself.

"Christ, I simply cannot believe this has happened. Cannot believe that boy is dead. Cannot believe Cassandra is dead! Dear God. It's too much to bear!"

"The boy was a student of yours?" Paul asked.

"Yes. Bradley Ruffin. A graduate student. Drama major. I was his academic advisor."

"Had he been in a lot of productions?" I asked.

"Oh, yes. I had directed several productions he was in. Brad was one of our more gifted, versatile students. Casting him was a simple matter. He was comfortable in dramas, had superb comedic timing. A voice that could convey passion, despair, irony. The boy had a future---as much as we can be certain anyone can have a future in the insane world of the theatre."

"He wanted a career in the theatre?" I asked. "Not planning to make it in Hollywood? Or television?"

He grimaced and shook his head vigorously.

"No, no! Not at all! Brad was serious about his work. Certainly he was charismatic, but he was not invested in the cult of personality. He wanted to continue learning his craft, studying acting. Over spring break, he was one of a dozen students we took to Stratford to see the Royal Shakespeare Company before rehearsals for *Henry V*. He planned to spend the summer here, part of a post-grad seminar I run with a few of our more advanced students. I think he had also enrolled in some classes in New York."

"You didn't know him outside of the theatre and classes?"

"I can't say I did."

"No beers after rehearsals?"

He shrugged. "Perhaps occasionally. Despite the school's liberal attitude, I think it better to maintain some reserve between myself and the students. If faculty become comrades we can hardly expect to be taken seriously when we critique students' performances. Not all of my colleagues agree, but that is my position. Naturally, we are available for conferences, for consultation---but as mentors, not as friends."

"How long have you been a teacher here?"

"Oh, hundreds of years!" He rolled his eyes, waving his hands dramatically.

55

"I began teaching here about twenty years ago, doing a semester now and then between shows. I worked Broadway and Off for many years. I was making a living, but was never going to be the greatest leading man of my generation, the new Brando, Pacino, deNiro, Spacey, take your pick. I had known Jason, our dear President, at school. We *prepped* together," he added with a note of sarcasm. "So I called him to see if he needed any part-time faculty. He was beefing up the drama department, so between gigs I began doing stints here at Bard---maybe teaching a senior seminar or a workshop---then I'd get cast in something in New York or pick up a part in a tour and wouldn't be here for months. Then I'd come back and teach Beckett for one term, Shakespeare for another. Eventually, as auditions dwindled, I stayed on. By that time, I discovered that I was a better teacher and director than actor." He smiled crookedly. "Our ability to rationalize separates us from the animals, you know."

"You were at the theatre before the show?"

"Of course! You don't think a curtain rises on a bloody thing like that without the director on hand? I was firmly planted in the wings, hissing commands."

"How often was Brad in the wings?"

"As I recall, his exits and entrances were from both sides of the stage. I didn't speak to him during the show except to tell him he was doing well and remind him to project." He paused. "This is such a terrible tragedy, a sad, sad accident."

Paul walked over to where I sat by deep French windows facing the Commons. We saw students crossing the lawn on their way to or from classes, others lounging on the grass in small groups, leaning on book satchels as they talked, laughed, or read to each other.

Turning back to face Palmer, Paul said, "This was no accident. Someone on that stage stabbed that boy."

Palmer's face fell. "Stabbed!? Murdered?!" he groaned. "You can't be serious?" He hid his face in his hands. "Murder most foul! Most foul, indeed! Dear God. I cannot believe it."

"Did Brad have any particular friends in the cast?"

"Isn't the more pertinent question 'Did he have any enemies?' " asked Palmer furiously.

"Why not tell us what you know about both?" Paul replied.

Palmer shrugged sadly. "I'm afraid I can't tell you that much. I only saw him in class and at rehearsals."

"The boy was killed on stage. He must have had some enemy in the cast or crew. Any problems during rehearsals? Any jealousies?"

"None that I noticed. As far as I could tell, the cast got on well. No one likes being passed over for a role but that happens all the time. If not getting cast in a part turned an actor into a killer, we'd never see any plays performed."

"Are you married?" I asked.

"No." He stood and leaned forward on his desk. "Should I assure you of my red-blooded manliness? Are you wondering if I killed Brad because he wouldn't act a certain part I had in mind for him?" He sat down with a great sigh. "Don't be absurd. I was fond of the boy, yes. But because I admired his talent."

Paul said, "Before I was sheriff, I was a farmer. Did you know cows can be bisexual? I figure the the-ah-tah offers people plenty of opportunities for, what shall we say, Lindsey?"

"---healthy ambiguity?" I suggested.

"---Right! And sex of one sort or another can figure in on a murder."

If Paul's ploy was to get a rise out of Palmer, it failed.

Paul handed him the *Henry V* program. "Why don't you suggest the people in the cast you think were closest to the boy."

Palmer circled one name and handed the program back. "He and one of his roommates, Elisabeth Johnson, were close, I think. I never noticed Brad being overly social with other students."

"Where did Brad live?" I asked.

"I've dropped him after rehearsals a time or two. He had a room in a house in Tivoli, a little place up the road. I couldn't tell you the exact address. My secretary can get that for you."

"What about his parents? Have you spoken to them?"

"Although I have met them several times, I have not seen them yet after last night's disaster. Jason wanted to see to that personally. After all, a lawsuit is the last thing he'd want, isn't it?"

"Let's hope finding the killer is the first thing."

As we stood, Paul said, "You'll be around for the next few weeks, correct? Not planning any field trips to Stratford?"

Palmer shook his head "No, I'm doing summer classes and workshops at the Music Festival."

"Good," Paul nodded. "We'll speak again."

As he held the door open for us to leave, Palmer said, "You can't honestly think I had anything to do with this awful tragedy. That's ridiculous. Please believe me."

Paul stopped and said, "I don't think anything one way or the other right now. What I do know is that someone on that stage killed that kid. I just need to find out who and why--- although, in my experience, not necessarily in that order."

AN APARTMENT IN TIVOLI

The village of Tivoli is less than ten minutes from Bard which makes it a popular spot for off-campus apartments. Several residential streets branch off the main drag. Most of the houses are simple 19th century summer houses or early 20th century bungalows.

What had once been a charming, tree-lined lane at the turn of the last century had devolved into a rather seedy neighborhood. A few eyebrow colonials were intact, barely, but could have been restored with relatively little effort and a few coats of paint. Other modest bungalows and cottages had been covered with fiberglass siding and, in one especially unfortunate case, baby blue asbestos shingles. A couple of large Victorian piles stood amid too-long grass and an assortment of barbecue grills and plastic yard furniture. Most of the houses were evenly set back about thirty feet from the street and displayed grimy porch boards and broken lattice work. Bicycles or tricycles lay in some yards, some porches had swings suspended on rusty chains. We parked in front of a house with faded yellow shutters and scraggles of low privet across the front and walked up a path bordered by leggy geraniums in coffee cans.

Our knock on the door went unanswered so Paul opened the screen door and called out.

His 'Anybody home?' brought a cry of 'Wait!' from upstairs and moments later a young woman came down the stairs clutching the banister in one hand and a black bandanna in the other. She was barefoot and was wearing a faded caftan. Her eyes were red and puffy from crying.

"Are you Elisabeth Johnson?"

She stared at him.

"Are you Elisabeth Johnson?"

"I am. Most people call me Eli."

"I'm Paul Whitbeck, the sheriff. This is my colleague, Lindsey Brooks. We're here about Brad Ruffin. Was he your roommate?"

"Roommate!" she gasped. "Who are you to call him that? He was more than a roommate! He was my soul, my rock!"

Paul glanced at me, then nodded, "Alright, Miss Johnson, Eli. I understand you are upset. But we need to talk to you about Brad's death. May we come in?"

The girl held the door open and gestured to a parlor on the left. We stepped inside. She led us through a bare front hall into a room decorated as a seraglio. Chairs had been covered in batiks. Tie-dyed curtains draped from the ceiling to form a tent in one corner. Two opposing walls were brilliant sapphire blue, the other two a rich pink. Potted palms sat in the corners by the large windows which stood open. Hinged wooden panels, roughly carved with trees and flowers, then painted, screened a doorway. I stood admiring the room.

The girl gestured at the screen. "It's good, isn't it? Brad and I carved the panels for last season's *Midsummer Night's Dream*. This room was done in the same spirit. I was Titania to his Oberon. It was a magical production. Did you see it?"

"Yes," I lied, "I did. It was marvelous. I adore ambiguous sexuality, don't you?"

She and Paul looked up sharply.

"What does that mean?" Elisabeth asked.

"My dear! Of course you realize that's a principal motif in *Misdsummer*! And there *was* some question about Brad's sexuality, wasn't there?" I sat down on the couch beside Paul and nudged his knee.

She tossed her head. "This is a tiny place, a small place. People talk. He was in love with me and not what some people made him out to be. Or wanted him to be, I can tell you that."

"Who would want to kill him?"

"No one wanted to kill him!" she shrieked. "It was a horrible accident!" She began to sob.

I moved to sit beside her on the ottoman and put my arm around her shoulder.

"Eli, the sheriff and I have to tell you that Brad's death was not an accident. He was stabbed. Someone on the stage killed him. You are going to help us find out who that was."

"Stabbed!" she cried. "But that arrow? I saw it in his chest."

After the wailing subsided, I began again.

"Never mind about the arrow. It was a knife, Eli. Someone had a knife and in the middle of the battle scene, they killed Brad. I'm sorry."

She managed to choke out, "But who would do that? Someone who begrudged him his success?"

Picking up on my tone, Paul asked, "His success on stage--- or his success with women? Or with men?"

She tossed her head, wiped the handkerchief furiously across her eyes and shot back, "He was an actor, all right? He could *act* different ways---doesn't mean he actually *was* a certain way because he acted like he was. You can *play* a king or a psychopath without *being* a king or a psychopath."

Paul asked, "How long have you been together?"

"Long enough to know we were going to be together forever."

"When did you meet?" I asked.

"Last year. We had several classes together and we had fabulous rapport when we were assigned some two-hand scenes."

"You say 'together forever.' Did he ever take you home to meet Mom and Dad?"

61

"Naturally! I met his parents several times when they came to see him in productions."

"Did you talk to Brad last night? How did he seem before the curtain rose?"

Pressing the bandanna to her eyes, she stood, fumbled in her pocket to extract a pack of cigarettes, lit one, then sank back onto the hassock.

"We didn't talk much, we were both busy getting ready. I worked this production as a wardrobe mistress. After getting the cast dressed, I stood in the wings, handing out spears and swords and shields. During the battle scene, some people rotated off, then reentered. That way, we made it look like more people. Actors would step into the wings, grab another spear and loft it."

"It's amazing to me that more people weren't injured. How did the arrows stay attached to people?" I asked.

"The arrows were easy. Everyone wore a muslin tunic padded with a layer of Styrofoam underneath. The arrows had guards about an inch up the shaft. They stuck in, but only so far."

"Must've been hell on the costumes," I murmured.

"It's stagecraft," she replied haughtily. "One learns these things."

"Had Brad antagonized anyone in the cast? Any hard feelings about his getting the part---instead of someone else?"

She burst into a fresh round of crying. "I don't know that he had any enemies."

Paul asked, "Did you notice anything unusual last night? Did you see anyone backstage you didn't recognize?"

She shook her head. "I...I don't think so. But I might not have noticed. Everyone was in costume so I wouldn't have been able to spot a stranger, really."

I asked, "Did women play some of the parts?"

She nodded. "Yes. But again, the audience wouldn't know that. Everyone wore a helmet or a visor and fake chain mail or tunics with hoods."

"We'd like to know more about the play that evening."

"What about it?"

"What exactly were you doing?"

"I told you. I was handing out spears."

"Could you be a little more specific? Let's start from when you arrived at the theatre."

She abruptly stood up and moved to another chair. "All right, I got in my car, the one that's in the driveway, and went to the theatre. First I went into make-up."

"Why make-up? I thought you were in the wings?"

"I was in the wings. But as I told you before, there was a lot of running on and off stage to make it seem like we had a bigger cast. Have you ever done theatre?"

"A bit. So what?" I asked.

"Have you ever seen a production of *The Chairs*?"

"Yes."

"Same thing. Several extras are costumed identically to the two leads. Their entrances and exits and the confusion are meant to suggest more people than there really are."

"Was Don Palmer overseeing all of this?"

"He didn't have to direct us that closely. We worked from sketches prepared by the designer and we'd rehearsed for a few weeks."

Paul asked, "Did you see the director before the show?"

She stopped and thought. "Yes, he was there."

"When did you first see him?"

"I can't say exactly when I first saw him. But I mightn't have noticed. There was so much going on. He was definitely there the entire time."

She paused. "I could tell he was slipping away from me."

"Brad? Slipping how?" I asked.

"We had talked about moving to the city together and going to auditions. But lately he had changed his mind. Said he

63

needed to be alone, to 'woo his Muse' was how he put it. He had decided to take private classes in the city."

"Were his parents amenable?"

"What do they have to do with it?"

"Presumably they would be paying for the lessons," I ventured. "Or did he plan to find work and make his own way?"

"He told me he had found a mentor, someone who took an interest in him."

"Who was that?" Paul asked. "Someone at the college?"

"He didn't say. He'd gotten very mysterious, like he didn't want me to latch onto him and try to tag along."

Paul persisted gently. "Eli, was it a man or a woman?"

"I don't know!" she said angrily. "Anyway, what possible difference does it make now?"

Paul stopped being solicitous. "Listen! You know, we're not writing a story for a tabloid, we're trying to find out who killed the boy," he snapped. "Withholding information could get you subpoenaed."

Her response was a shrug. "I told you. I don't know."

Seeing we were stalled for the moment, Paul said, "We'll need to see his room."

"Sure," she said and led us up the stairs. There were two bedrooms on the second floor with a shared bath. The walls of the landing were covered with photographs of Olivier, Ian MacKellan, Gielgud, Diana Rigg, Francesca Annis, Geraldine McEwan, Maggie, Judi, Derek Jacobi.

"What's this rogue's gallery?" I asked

"They are the greats, the ones we must emulate," she answered. "They gave their lives to the theatre and their audiences."

"Who put these up?"

"Brad did."

"A surprisingly older crowd for someone his age," I observed. "What about contemporary actors?"

"Brad was old beyond his years. He valued the history of the theatre---and the wisdom of the classics."

Paul looked down at his watch and said, "Miss Johnson, thank you for talking to us. We'll be in touch. We need to look at Brad's room now. You're free to go."

She nodded. "I understand," she said. "Just close the door when you leave. I'm going out for a walk."

◆◆◆◆◆

Paul observed, "He played a lot of roles, that boy. Son. Boyfriend. Maybe gigolo. But he excelled at his last part---a corpse. What we need is a motive. Was it a lovers' quarrel that got out of hand? Was he leaving her for another woman? A man? Who was his patron?"

"And," I added, "what if anything did that death have to do with Cassandra?"

Paul frowned. "Cassandra? I can't see any connection at all. A kid gets stabbed and a woman has a heart attack. What does one have to do with the other? We don't even know if they knew each other."

"No, we don't, but I think we should find out if they did."

Opening the door to Brad's room, we found a bed, neatly made, covered with a navy duvet. Bookshelves lined one wall. Another wall held a pier mirror. An armoire stood between two windows facing the back yard.

His desk was piled with books, several scripts, and a calendar. Paul began going through drawers while I examined the armoire. Among the usual jeans, cords, and chinos, there were a few sportcoats, several denim shirts, and a tux. I began going through all the pockets.

The inside pocket of a blazer held a used Amtrak ticket to New York dated two weeks before. The side pocket held a scrap of paper with a phone number.

"This is interesting," Paul said, walking over with a diary. "Two weeks ago he had an appointment in Hudson, says here 520 Warren Street."

"What's there?"

"City Hall."

"Huh."

Paul and I spent a few more minutes riffling through desk drawers. Then he said, "You and I are done here. I'll send my sergeants over to make a more complete search. Let's go."

As we walked back to Paul's car, I asked, "What did you make of her?"

"Well," Paul laughed and shoved his hands into his pockets. "To be honest, I spent the first few minutes persuading myself that it was really a she."

"Yeah, I know," I answered. Smallest breasts ever. Hardly there at all. Androgenous physique, slim, slim hips. And not a strictly feminine face, not conventionally pretty. When her face is animated, she is interesting-looking in a street waif, gamine sort of way, but in repose? A rather disturbing face. Lots of emotion dammed up behind it. It will be interesting to get her back story.

"Could she have done it?" I asked.

Paul answered, "It's for damn sure she had the opportunity. And behind all those tears, she's mad as hell---the guy was getting ready to dump her. I wouldn't rule her out."

QUESTIONS IN THE VILLAGE OF TIVOLI

Tivoli's main street recalls the 1960s with Peace and Love Cafes, funky dress shops and restaurants, an organic bakery, and storefronts in two- or three-storey Victorian brick buildings with apartments on the upper floors. The place has about 1,200 residents and thirty years ago you could have bought the entire town for $25,000.

Several years ago the Madalin Hotel opened and immediately became a hot spot for locals and local worthies. Two brothers from New York and a pal quit being trial lawyers and opened a B&B serving delicious food and inventive cocktails in what had been an old roadhouse on the main drag.

As a roadhouse it featured a memorably shabby bar populated by losers, loners, and college kids having 35 cent beers at the long bar. I definitely miss that joint but it is nice to find a decent dinner equidistant between Rhinebeck and Hudson.

The new Madalin bar has cool photography plus two television sets tuned to sports channels, and attracts a big happy hour crowd. Across the hall, the dining room is more formal and, like the bar, is full most nights in the winter. Late spring, summer, and autumn dining moves outside onto a broad veranda, the perfect place to watch the local world go by.

Paul and I found the parents seated on that veranda. Dottie, in a beige sheath and sunglasses, had aged since I met her a few days ago. While she fidgeted with several gold bangles, her husband, Louis, sitting opposite her, stared out into the street with vacant eyes. Despite the heat, he was wearing a suit with the tie firmly knotted. Neither looked as though they had slept.

After expressing our regrets about their loss, Paul began, "Tell us about Brad."

Dottie said, "He was always a good kid, decent student, imaginative, creative. Never gave us any trouble."

"I suppose most people would call us a happy family," Louis said.

"Do you have other children?" Paul asked.

Louis shook his head. "No. Only Brad."

"How long have you been together? How did you meet?" I asked.

"We met in high school in Memphis and married at nineteen. We went to college together, in New Haven. Dottie took time off when Brad arrived and I continued with school. After graduation, I studied in Philadelphia."

"What were you studying?" I asked.

"Architecture."

"Do you do residential, commercial, what?"

"I've done it all. I have a firm in Greenwich."

"How about you, Dottie?" I asked.

"After Brad started putting in a full day at grammar school, I went back to college part-time, finished my undergraduate, then enrolled in law school. I, too, have a firm in Greenwich."

"What kind of law?" I asked.

"Mostly contracts. Some civil, real estate, an occasional divorce. "

"The O'Connells used to live in Connecticut. Did you know them?"

"Don't believe we did. Were they in Greenwich?" asked Dottie.

"Green Farms," I answered.

"Oh, wait." Louis spoke up. "I think they did contact our firm at one point. Wanted to put an addition on their house. It never worked out."

"Why not?"

"Just very different aesthetics. They wanted something modern, our work has a more classical vocabulary."

"I see. How did Brad choose Bard?"

"At the time, we both tried to talk him out of it. He'd already done his BA and the most obvious thing was to move on to Yale Drama. He'd have been a shoo-in. But he was dead set on making his own way. Bard has a reputation of being a creative hotbed. And while they do have a good faculty, it's not New Haven." His voice trailed off. "Not that my opinion would have swayed him."

Dottie began to cry a little bit. "But, Louis, he seemed happy here, though."

"How often did you see Brad?" Paul asked.

His father handed his wife his handkerchief. "We saw him at Easter, of course, and when he came over for Mother's Day."

"Were his classes going well? Did he mention any problems?" I asked.

"No," Dottie answered. "In fact, he seemed to be on top of the world. He liked his teachers, he liked the drama workshops and stage productions."

"Had you seen many of his productions?"

"I've seen all of them," Dottie said.

Dottie continued, "We met with Don Palmer, his faculty advisor, earlier this year. He told us Brad was doing very well, that he had a bright future."

Louis added, "I had a meeting in Albany a week or so ago and stopped by to watch a dress and tech rehearsal for this play. We had dinner afterward and in his conversation, there was one thing that worried me a bit," Louis said. "He seemed to be under the sway of someone, a teacher maybe, who I guess was giving him private acting lessons. He had become very secretive about his plans after graduation."

"Secretive how?" I asked.

"He didn't want us to have to support him any longer. Felt it was time for him to grow up. I pointed out that our parents had supported us while we got through school and until we could earn a living on our own. It wasn't like he was supplied with unlimited amounts of cash. He had a budget."

"Met any of his friends?" I asked.

Dottie answered, "Yes, we have, but very casually." They looked at each other.

"Not really. I mean, we may have met a few," Louis answered.

"Have you met his roommate?" Paul asked.

Louis said, "Last term he was in a house with three or four kids splitting the rent. This year he moved in with a girl. We met her, I think, maybe once, I can't recall. All students look alike."

Paul leaned forward on his elbows. "What do you think happened to Brad last night?"

His mother began to cry again.

His father snorted, "Apparently he caught an arrow in his chest. If it had been me, and if that hadn't killed me, I might have had a heart attack."

Paul nodded. Continuing along that line, which I still did not quite understand, Paul asked, "Is there a family history of heart issues? Did he have an arrhythmia? Any mitral valve problems? Childhood illnesses? Rheumatic fever?"

"No family history that is relevant in the least," Père Ruffin snapped. "Are you suggesting we need to have an autopsy? I know you took my son's body away last night because you viewed it, I gather, as a suspicious death. Why you feel that way, I cannot imagine. You need to have some respect for his mother and me. As I said to Jason when we met him this morning, we don't want to make a federal case out of this! Brad is dead and whether he died of a stroke, a seizure, an arrow, whatever, is of no real interest to us. He's gone! All of this after

70

the fact, Monday morning diagnosis is useless! Can't you understand we want to bury him with dignity? We don't even know where his damned body is at this moment! Why don't you fill us in on that?!"

Paul answered, "We did take your son's body away, to the medical examiner. I am sorry to tell you this but your son did not die of an arrow wound or of natural causes. Someone stuck a knife in him. He was murdered in full view of you, me, and the entire audience."

DOCTOR VANCE'S MANNER

Our next stop was Dr. William Vance, the doctor who ran to the stage the night of *Henry V*.

Following his pronouncement of Brad Ruffin's death, he had raced back to the seats to examine Cassandra after she collapsed. At that time we learned he was, in fact, her doctor.

Vance's office is in a wood frame house off Route 9 on the border of Red Hook and Rhinebeck. Vance was a Jack Lemmon lookalike whose face had seen better days. He wore a navy blazer over a blue shirt with frayed cuffs and rumpled chinos. A speck of egg sat in the middle of his tie.

"Cause of death?" Paul asked. "Your professional opinion?"

"Stroke or cardiac arrest."

"How do you know?" I asked.

"Medical expertise, my dears! Don't forget, she *was* my patient. The lady was a certain type---a major hypochondriac. Told me she always consulted a doctor immediately whenever she relocated. Cassandra came to see me first thing when she got up here. Worried about allergies, worried about Lyme disease, worried about Swine Flu, you name it. Even asked if I could do DNA tests that show likelihood of diseases. Wanted me to do a complete workup," Vance chuckled, "and then take her to lunch! Quite a flirt."

He gave us a man-about-town wink. As I squirmed in my seat, Paul snapped, "And so then what?"

Vance continued, "Anyway, I ran an EKG, did blood work, the usual battery of tests. Nothing particularly unusual except she had a heart murmur and an irregular heartbeat. No different from 20 percent of the population. Her condition was not grave, at least I thought not. But arrhythmias are funny. Anything could have triggered a major event. My guess? The excitement of the evening, the hullabaloo processional, the commotion on stage, the sudden call for a doctor, but it could have been…anything, really. Or all of that at once."

"The only way to be sure is with an MRI or a full post-mortem. But you aren't planning an autopsy, surely, Sheriff?"

"Probably not," Paul said, glancing at me.

Vance shrugged.

"Well, it's your call. But I think it is pretty obvious that she simply died. After all, the woman was, as they say, of a certain age"---he consulted a file---"in her mid- fifties, according to what she told me. Not that that is true, mind you. Look, this is not a statistical aberration. Besides which, unless you are coming right out and saying the death is suspicious, to get an autopsy you'll need a next of kin. Do you know who that might be?"

Paul looked at me.

"I don't know," I said. "I'll ask Huxley."

Paul said, "We'll keep her on ice. I'll get back to you."

As we walked to the car, I said, "I think you ought to order an autopsy."

Paul grimaced. "Damn it, Lindsey, I know you think that. But think for a minute about what that means. Instead of one murder, we'll have two murders. Do you want all the parents hauling their kids out of that college? Is that what you want?"

"Of course not. But I do think there is too much of a coincidence. Two murders within a few hundred feet of each other."

"Not murders, Lindsey, deaths. Big difference."

"All you need to order an autopsy is a suspicion of foul play, that's all. Why don't you order one, then we'll know."

Paul sighed. "Fine! You go to the funeral home and let them know my office will be calling. But I am telling you now, the funeral director is going to release this to the press and then all hell is going to break loose."

Paul went to confer with his deputies and I headed off to collect Huxley.

"Who would be Cassandra's next of kin?" I asked as I barged into the butler's pantry where Huxley was deboning a chicken.

"I'd say no one," Huxley answered, wiping his hands on a towel. "She was an only child. Any of her parents' siblings would be long gone. As for distant cousins, hell, who gives a damn about cousins and we'd never find them anyway."

"Put that knife down and get in the car."

"Yes, madame," Hux answered.

Cassandra's body was at the local funeral home.

The mortuary in Rhinebeck stands on the main street in a grove of sugar maples. Originally a family residence, it is a modified version of the Hudson bracketed style---a white clapboard center hall with wings on either side and gray shutters on the windows. The pretty old place could easily have become a B&B but instead the parlors are now viewing rooms and I entered to find two visiting periods in full swing. An unctuous fellow in a gray suit asked which book we'd like to sign---the Wilder or the Mazerella.

"I'm Lindsey Brooks and this is Huxley Smythe. We are here to see the mortician about Cassandra Chappelle."

The receptionist looked as though she'd been stabbed. "The correct term is funeral director," she said icily, "You may wait here."

"Whatever," I responded glumly.

Huxley and I sat in the beige-carpeted, beige-painted central foyer, waiting, beside a table on which lay a Gideon bible, a *Highlights for Children* and the latest issue of *Martha Stewart Living*. Pretty much all one needs, cradle to grave, I thought. I considered reading through the Psalms, thought of browsing Martha's recipes, but elected to find the hidden objects in the trees and bushes of a *Highlights* exercise. There were supposed to be fifteen; I had found ten when a man approached.

"Miss Brooks, Mr. Smythe?" he inquired.

Huxley and I stood.

"I'm Raymond Caulbere. I'm the funeral director. You are here about Miss Chappelle. Shall we step into my office?"

Mr. Caulbere was six feet tall, slightly hunched, and slightly sallow with dampish, lank brown hair. His eyebrows were enormous, bristling things. He wore the requisite black serge suit and a black tie. Central casting.

As we walked down the hall, he asked, "Am I correct that you are here to discuss arrangements for the funeral?"

Huxley spoke up. "Yes. We'd like elephants."

I glanced at him and frowned.

"Mr. Smythe was a close friend and is perhaps not himself," I said to the funeral director---although I knew Huxley was very much himself.

We entered his office. Mr. Caulbere turned, and closed the door behind us.

"Before I hear what you have come to say, I must tell you something. I will not embalm the body. I am of the opinion an autopsy should be performed."

"You are?" I asked, startled. "Why?"

"I believe the woman was murdered."

Huxley swore and sat down very heavily.

"Why do you say that?" he rasped.

"Let's just say it is a feeling I have. Does my name mean anything to you?"

" 'Caulbere,' " I murmured. "I can't say it does, really," I answered.

Huxley spoke up. "Doesn't it have something to do with witches---no, not witches exactly, but something about the middle ages? Magicians? Seers? I can't quite recall..."

The mortician continued.

"Hundreds of years ago my family was given the name 'Caulbere' because the women in my family often bore children whose faces were swathed in cauls, that is, newborns enveloped in the amniotic sac at birth. A highly unusual, and some would say, disturbing, phenomenon. Such children were said to have certain powers, to foresee the future, to divine mysteries. Charlemagne, Napoleon, Freud, and Lord Byron were born with cauls. Holden Caulfield is an allusion to this type of birth. Dickens prescribed that David Copperfield was born with a caul.

"And, often to my sadness, I do seem to be able to divine things which are not obvious. Since this unfortunate woman's body was brought here, I have felt certain her passing was not only untimely but had been planned. She was executed."

An hour later, Cassandra's body was transferred to the coroner's office.

PERUSAL OF CASSANDRA'S OFFICE

Since Huxley was the person who had known Cassandra longest---indeed, was the only person who knew her at all, aside from Franklin---it seemed logical to take him into my confidence.

"I, too, have been lobbying for an autopsy," I ventured after we had left Caulbere and drove up 9G north to Cassandra's house.

"Why?" he asked. "Like everybody else, I assumed she died of shock or a dicky ticker, as they say in Knightsbridge."

I shook my head.

"No, I don't think so, not that tough bird. No, you've told me the woman was hard as nails, you've told me she was indomitable. She was not the sort to keel over at a theatrical mishap. I think someone wanted her out of the way and I expect the autopsy is going to prove me right."

"But how could she have been killed, Lindsey? We were with her every minute that evening."

"I don't know how she was killed, Huxley, but I think she was. What I'd like you to help me do is figure out who would have benefitted from her death."

"Yes, the will. We need her will," Huxley murmured.

"Exactly."

"Huxley, I am afraid I have something else to tell you."

"Yes, my dear?"

"Cassandra was conniving to get Franklin away from Francesca."

"What!" Huxley shouted. "What a ridiculous idea! I'm aware that she flirted with him like mad but she flirted with any male, every male. Flirting was like breathing to her. You're jumping to conclusions."

"Huxley, she *told me* those were her plans. And I think Francesca had figured that out."

Huxley grimaced. "Which would give Francesca a motive? Oh, dear. This is going to get sticky."

We drove up to Cassandra's house. The housekeeper was there to let us in.

I always make a point of knowing the names of friends' staffs and ingratiating myself with them. This knowledge is often useful at parties and comes in particularly handy when you're trying to find a dead friend's will. The maid's name was Magda. She was vaguely Hungarian. She was shortish with a wiry build and dark pewter hair pulled savagely back into severe buns on either side of her head. She wore a white pinafore apron over a starched dark gray shirtwaist.

"Magda," I said, taking her hands in mine, "Mr. Smythe and I are terribly sorry about Miss Chappelle. I know it must have been a great shock to you."

Magda said in mournful tones, "Somevon kilt her. Ven you find out who it vas, *I'm* going to kill *him*."

Huxley and I didn't dare look at each other. In less than thirty minutes two people had told us Cassandra had been murdered.

Still, to preserve appearances since we actually did not know that for sure, I said, "Magda, the examining doctor---her own physician, as it happens---believes Miss Chappelle had a heart attack brought on by shock."

"Quatsch! Rubbitsch! She vas kilt."

"Magda, may we look around? We may discover something that will help us figure this out what has actually happened."

Following Magda through the living room, shortly we were ensconced in Cassandra's office. It held a large desk, a wall of filing cabinets, various upholstered chairs, a chintz swathed ottoman, a large flat screen, and a computer on a drop leaf table.

"How did Cassandra seem to you? Was she worried about anything?"

"Not vorried so much as trying to figure out who vas who!" Magda intoned ominously.

"What does that mean?" Huxley asked.

"Several men vere calling on her. Some vere hextremely young. She vas vain! Vain! She thought they vere courting but any fool except an old fool could see they vere more interested in her checkbook than her knickers."

"How young?"

"Too young. She vas an old fool."

"We need to find her will. Any idea where that might…"

Magda snorted, "Her vill?! Vich one?! She changed her vill every other veek."

"How do you know that?" I asked. "Did she ask you to witness it?"

Magda nodded vigorously. "Every time she changed it, I vas to vatch while she signed it, then sign it myself. Vonce every veek or two, I vould say."

"Are you aware of what the changes were?"

Magda snorted and shook her head. "Of course not! She just needed me to vitness her signature, she didn't let me read the thing. But sometimes she'd say enough so that I'd get the gist of vhat vas up. This von 'vill need money for his studio classes. He is such a talent.' This von 'needs all the help he can get to escape the boorzhvah existence his parents have planned for him.' Vot is boorzhvah?"

"That," intoned Huxley, "is a matter of continuing debate."

"Did you hear any of her conversations with these young men?"

"Only snatches. It hass been such luffly vedther since Cass, that is, Miss Chappelle, got here, she did most of her receiving on the terrace. I vould bring tea or cocktails and then get lost. Eef dey came for dinner, I vould set table, put food in varming oven. And then get lost."

"Do you know the names of the men who came?"

She shook her head. "Vonce I heard her scream and vhen I ran outside they had their arms around each other and she vas saying, 'Oh Darlink! You are the von! I knew it from the moment I saw you!' That vas the yung von. And then there vas the doctor. She called him 'the doctor of love'. He vould arrive for drinks and the first thing he vould say vas, 'oh, you look so lovely, but to be sure I must listen to your heart.' He vould not use a stethoscope, if you see vot I mean. I don't zink I ever heard her use der real names."

Huxley and I exchanged frowns.

"And you think one of her suitors killed her?" I asked.

"Ja, I do."

"Magda, when Cassandra was here alone, where did she sit? Say, when she was watching television or reading?"

"She sat right there in that chair vith her feet on the ottoman."

I sat in the chair and put my feet up. Scanning the room, I said, "I'm thinking she would have wanted to have the hiding place in view."

"Magda," I said, "Mr. Smythe and I are going to go through Miss Chappelle's office to see if we find anything in her papers to shed light on this. If we need you, we'll call you."

Magda nodded. "Start vith the desk. The vill has to be in this rhoom somevere."

She made for the door and threw over her shoulder a final remark, "I hope you'll recognize any other clooz ven you see dem."

Huxley watched Magda head down the hall, then closed the door.

"So Cassandra was entertaining gentlemen callers! Young suitors! And 'The Doctor of Love,' no less! How does that square with her setting her sights on Franklin?" I wondered aloud.

"Darling," Huxley replied, "you are a woman. Do you honestly intend to tell me that you have never hedged your bets in the lovers' sweepstakes?"

Nodding, I said, "Yes, I see your point. Still, I believed she genuinely cared for Franklin---*and* she said she intended to get him, come hell or high water."

"Lindsey, each year you become more naïve. By December, I expect to find you lying in a manger. Yes, Cassandra was ruthless and if, as you say, she had set her sights on Franklin, which she never told me, by the way, then she would have gone to any length to get him away from Francesca. However, Cassandra was also a realist. She knew a worthy adversary when she saw one and Francesca on the battlefield would make Attila blanch. My guess is she allowed herself to be seduced---some would say serviced---by a few younger---and older---lads until she saw how the Franklin thing would play out. No harm in that. Except she's dead, of course." Huxley frowned again.

I shook my head. "But if I were a gigolo, why would I kill the goose that was laying the golden egg? Murdering one's patron does not a successful career path make."

"If Magda's blathering about the will is true, and if others knew about provisions made for them, perhaps it was a matter of her being more valuable to someone dead than alive?"

Huxley sat down in front of a canvas filled with interlocking blue and green rectangles. "I wonder if the Marlborough has seen this."

"One of her paintings?" I asked.

He nodded. "Look around. They're all like this. She spent a fortune on painting lessons. Always painted geometric shapes. Once, before she moved to California, when we were having drinks in her loft in the Village, I suggested to her there was a wonderful new invention, fruit. Couldn't she paint a pear, for God's sake, or a pile of mangoes or some grapes? She said she wanted to paint the inside of her mind. Now *that* would have been a portrait in miniature."

"Huxley, you sound like a scorned suitor. Was there something between you and Cassandra that never went anywhere?"

"My dear, even if I had been interested, and may I assure you I was not, I was never wealthy enough for Cassandra. Her childhood was dreadful. Father extinguished by a drunk driver when she was a tot, plunging the family into penury. The ultimate stage mother controlled her every move and forced her to perform---spending every dime they had on voice, dance, elocution lessons from the age of five. She and I were in a grocery store once and she picked up a can of Spam and did her Vivian Leigh 'As God is my witness, I'll never be hungry again' speech, then laughed and threw it back."

"Let's find her will."

The desk was a large roll top affair with a cliff of cubbyholes. The woman was a packrat. Her desk was crammed with receipts, bills, letters, lists, some ancient, others recent. God only knew what was in the file cabinets. I felt tired already.

Cassandra had used a business-style ledger checkbook and each entry was thoroughly annotated. Several payments were made to Freeman & Hehmeyer. Some correspondence on letterhead showed they were attorneys in Ojai. I rang Paul; the time zone difference made it possible for him to call their offices immediately and get the ball rolling.

My phone rang back promptly with Paul's report. "They say they are the attorneys for just about anything she does and that she made out a will before she headed East. She signed it in their offices and left with a copy so it must be there. Is there a safe?" Paul sounded harried.

"No safe yet and no will in the desk. A damned phalanx of file cabinets is next. I'll keep looking."

When I told you she was a packrat, I understated it. All the files were more or less labeled but there were hundreds of them. Recipes, stubs from movies, old scraps of fabrics, leases, correspondence. While Huxley busied himself going through another cabinet, I took every painting off the wall to look for a safe. No luck.

We took the bed apart, flipped the mattress, shone a flashlight underneath.

I stomped on floorboards trying for a secret compartment. I looked through every purse and briefcase. I emptied every drawer and looked on the bottoms.

After two hours, Huxley barked, "This is tiresome. Why can't we just get a copy from the lawyers?"

"Because unless she sent them copies every time she changed it, their file copy is several generations old. No, I'm betting the last copy, witnessed by Magda, is in this room somewhere. You and I are going to go through her papers, look for a will and see if we can figure out who stands to gain from her death.

"We'll start again tomorrow."

By the time I dropped Huxley at his house and trundled back to my place, the Martini Alarm was blaring in my brain.

Bennett met me in the driveway with a salver of libations and a single rosebud in a tiny vase. This is why it's good to have a man around the house. We strolled over to a garden bench, said cheers, smiled, and I took a big swallow.

"Dinner is all ready. I had thought we might dine al fresco? So all you have to do is relax---*and tell me everything, madame!* Don't skip over the good spots!"

"The operative phrase appears to be Gentlemen Callers. All ages, all sizes."

"Such as?"

"Her doctor, for one. The maid never got anyone's name, so that makes the IDs a tad tricky. I'm thinking the dead kid had been coming around but I can't figure out how they would have met."

Bennett said. "Well, they both were at Huxley's party that afternoon."

"No, this would have been going back for weeks. His girlfriend, or roommate, whichever or both, said that he had found a wealthy patron. Could have been Cassandra. If not, who else?"

"Is the autopsy is going forward?"

"Oh, yes. In addition to my insistence, the mortician, name of Caulbere…"

"Oh, dear," said Bennett.

"…is certain she was murdered. He had a vision or something. Anyhow, let's have another drink and then I've got some reading for us to do over dinner."

I retrieved a fat file labeled Upcoming Auctions and Estate Sales.

"Mustn't allow murders to intrude upon our livelihood."

CASSANDRA'S AUTOPSY

Our coroner's office is in the new county office building. The morgue is in the basement. Getting there one passes bulletin boards advertising day care, long benches with those on the county dole waiting to see an official, and a plethora of clerks conducting county business.

The new morgue is more streamlined than the old one, but the paraphernalia of death remains the same. There's the antiseptic tang. The same scuffed Steelcase desks and file cabinets, the same cold, hard, metal tables, and stainless steel trays of ghastly instruments---bone saws, rib cutters, scalpels, needles, skull chisels, and very long knives. There's an entire wall of refrigerators and freezers. White tiled counters and cabinets line the remaining walls.

Cassandra's physician, William Vance, had asked to be present for the coroner's report.

While we waited on the coroner, Vance intoned, "Sheriff, I have to tell you both again. It was a heart attack, pure and simple---or a stroke. She was not an old woman, per se, but neither was she a spring chicken. Nothing at all out of the ordinary. The woman was with you the entire evening, at drinks, dinner, and the ride over to the theatre. I'm not sure why you are viewing this as a suspicious death in the first place."

"I guess it seemed too much of a coincidence that we had two people die that night within minutes of each other," I said.

The medical examiner, Frank Carver entered. No need to remark on his name.

Paul said, "Lindsey, you and Frank know each other."

"Hello, again, Dr. Carver," I said. We shook hands.

"Hello, again, Lindsey. Morning, Paul."

Carver is a distinguished-looking man with a great shock of auburn hair gone deeply gray at the temples. His freckled hands and forearms are thick with reddish hair. He wore a lab coat open with the sleeves pulled up, a blue shirt and chinos, and a subdued green paisley tie.

Paul said, "Frank, this is Dr. William Vance, the deceased's physician."

"Good morning, Dr. Vance," Carver said.

As they shook hands, Dr. Vance quickly spoke up, "The blood tests told the tale, eh?"

Eyebrows raised, Dr. Carver nodded, "Oh, yes. Definitely told the tale."

For our edification, Vance continued, "Dying heart muscles release cardiac enzymes, proteins, into the bloodstream. These cardiac enzymes are elevated in the blood several hours after the onset of a heart attack. Or in a stroke, you've got hemorrhagic evidence on the brain. So is that what you found, Carver? That the old girl just keeled over?"

Carver looked at each of us in turn as he nodded his head. "You've got that much right, Vance. She certainly did keel over. She had a heart attack, not a stroke."

Vance nodded sagely.

Carver said, "Why don't we all sit down and I'll go over our findings."

We walked out of the morgue theatre and into his office. Dr. Carver sat down at his desk and consulted the notes on his clipboard as the rest of us found chairs or sank into the Naugahyde sofa.

"However," he continued, adjusting his glasses, "I'm afraid it's not as simple as that. A heart attack, yes. But I am sorry to tell you that it was not a 'natural' heart attack, per se."

"How do you mean?" Paul asked.

"This woman's heart attack was triggered by a substantial amount of poison."

"Poison?!" Vance cried, jumping up. "What the hell are you saying?"

"I'm saying her stomach contained several teaspoons of aconite."

"Monk's Hood," I said. "I have a garden full of it."

Carver continued. "Aconite disrupts the ion balance in heart muscle cells, causing potentially fatal arrhythmias, including ventricular tachycardia---an excessively rapid heartbeat---producing a heart attack. That is what killed her."

Carver asked, "Were you with her at the O'Connells', Lindsey?"

"Yes, Paul and I were both at her table at dinner. Afterward she drove to the theatre with us."

"Well, she would have ingested the aconite two hours---at the most---before she died. Did she complain of any stomach cramps, nausea, or any numbness in her mouth or tongue?"

"She did mention that the wine at dinner might not have agreed with her," I said. "Or that she might have had one glass of wine too many, said she felt rather light-headed. And several times she said she felt very excited, not surprising---we were at a gala dinner and she was the honoree. But generally she seemed fine."

Paul asked, "Would the poison have acted that fast?"

Carver nodded. "The symptoms come on very quickly. With that amount of aconite in her system, she could have felt quite unwell, she might even have vomited."

"I heard no complaints. Paul, am I not remembering something important?"

Paul shook his head. "She chattered the entire way. If she was not feeling well, she gave no sign."

"Of course, the woman was an actress," I said, "and as the benefactor for the production, she was very much in the spotlight that evening. With her training she could have simply put on a smiling face and ignored what she took to be a case of indigestion.

"And the play opened with so much commotion, we wouldn't have noticed any agitation on her part during the first act, especially after the lights lowered."

We sat staring at each other as the fact of Cassandra's murder sank in.

"What happens to Miss Chappelle now?" Carver asked, turning to me.

"According to Huxley," I answered, "she wanted to be cremated with her ashes scattered in the Pacific Ocean."

"Whatever happened to her child, I wonder?" mused Dr. Carver.

"Cassandra had no children," I said.

"Well, she had a caesarian scar. So at least she had a delivery."

As we walked to our cars, I said, "Dr. Vance, would you characterize your relationship with Cassandra as strictly medical practitioner and patient?"

"What exactly do you mean by 'strictly'?"

"I understood you might be characterized as gentleman caller, that you were a frequent guest."

"Oh, for heaven's sake! There's no harm in two adults seeing each other on a purely social basis. What's the big deal? I took Cass to dinner a few times and she had me over occasionally. We amused each other. For heaven's sake, don't listen to that gorgon of a housekeeper of hers! She's from the Black Forest. To her everyone is an ogre."

FINDING THE POISON

The news that Cassandra had been poisoned pointed us back to the O'Connells'. She had obviously ingested the aconite at dinner.

As we drove to the O'Connells', Paul said, "You did a lot of nodding about the aconite. Are you now an expert on poisons?"

I shook my head.

"Hardly an expert, dear. But any reasonably informed gardener would know that Monk's Hood *is* poison. Every part of it---leaves, stalks, blooms, roots. So many common plants *are* poisonous---datura, brugmansia, baptisia, columbine, foxglove---even poor old rhododendron and daffodils will kill you if you eat enough of the right parts. But aconite is especially potent, so potent the Germans used it for poison bullets in World War II. Ancient Greeks put it on their arrows."

"Jesus!" Paul exclaimed. "Does it grow around here?"

"Paul, almost every garden in the Valley has Monk's Hood. It's a favorite perennial in the back of the border because of its height—usually five to six feet tall---and because it blooms for a few weeks. Francesca has some aconite I gave her last year when I divided the patch at Bennett's cottage. I'll show you when we go to the O'Connells'."

Then I thought, 'Oops,' as Paul cocked his eyebrow and said, "Do tell."

Paul continued, "I'm going to send my guys over to the O'Connells first, get the details on the food preparation, the service, the whole nine yards. Let's see if we turn up anything interesting. The poison had to be on the woman's plate that night."

♦♦♦♦♦

What Paul's deputies may have lacked in experience on a suspicious death inquiry they more than made up for in thoroughness and efficiency as they pursued lines of inquiry.

Twenty-four hours later they had gleaned from Francesca an enormous amount of information on the party that night. The food---every course, every ingredient---was documented, as were the catering chefs and the servers, as well as whoever among Francesca's own staff had worked the party, and the guest list.

Reviewing their findings with me, Paul said, "I'm so pleased with the initiative these young fellows have shown! Aren't you impressed?!"

"Yes, I am," I agreed. "They got a great deal done in a remarkably short time."

I also thought about how thrilled Francesca would have been at being interrogated by police officers in her own home.

Grabbing his suit jacket, Paul said, "Good, now step lively. You and I are going over all the details with Mrs. O'Connell ourselves, make sure they didn't miss anything.

"Come along, dear."

Discussing Dinner with Francesca

As I normally do when arriving at the O'Connells', I opened the front door and walked in, calling, "Francesca! I'm home!"

This time however, instead of the usual effusive greeting, I got a chilly reception. Traveling with the Sheriff can play hell with one's Trendex.

"Come in here," were Francesca's opening words as she led us through the gallery and into the living room, a 3000-square-foot parlor that can double as a ballroom after the furniture is dispatched by the village of Guatemalans.

"What is it you want?" Francesca asked as she sat down, glaring at us.

"Thanks so much for receiving us," I said, trying to offset her obvious hostility with a note of civility.

Paul added, "Yes, we appreciate it. I'd like to go over the dinner that evening."

Francesca interrupted sharply, "You must be joking! I've been over that nine times with your deputies. I've answered hundreds of questions. What can I possibly add!? I have a meeting in twenty minutes and a massage after that. So if you can get whatever else you think you need in that time frame, great."

Paul gave her a thin smile. "Absolutely, Mrs. O'Connell, we'll move right along. We'd like to go over the organization of the party, the flow of the evening and the food."

Francesca said, "I went over all of this yesterday ad nauseam with your people! And you were there that evening, for God's sake! Why didn't you pay more attention? And what does my food have to do with her heart attack?"

Paul said, "The doctors seem to think something she ate killed her. She ate here."

Francesca stared open-mouthed. "She died because of something she ate? But everyone *ate the same things*---and no one else died! What the hell are you driving at?"

"Just take us through the planning, would you? We don't want to make you late for that massage." Paul smiled again. "Or, after you're more refreshed, you could come to my office and we could talk there." Again he smiled. Francesca abruptly stood up, talking over her shoulder as she strode toward the door.

"The menu had, of course, been planned for weeks. They pre-cook most things, then bring the food here to finish or to be warmed. That's all in the kitchen."

"Then let's start there," I suggested.

Bristling with exasperation, Francesca led us back through the gallery, past the Avedon and Arbus photographs, the Rivers and Malevich paintings, and several sculptures.

She pushed open swinging doors and we entered what could have been, by its size, a restaurant kitchen. Four double ovens, two professional Garland stoves, three double fridges, several dishwashers, and enough cabinets and counter space for a home store, all in off-white wood and pale green granite.

Many of the cabinets were glass-fronted and held forests of stemware---wine glasses for bordeaux, burgundy, Pinot Noir, Sauvignon Blanc, Montrachet, ports, flutes and bells. All labeled. Clearly this household entertained on a grand scale---and frequently.

"The caterers set up in here." Francesca said.

"How does the food get here?" Paul asked.

"THEY BRING IT IN VANS!" Francesca yelled.

"Walk me through it, would you?" Paul smiled.

"Jesus Mary and Joseph!" said Francesca. She led us out of the kitchen, through another door, back into a hallway, past the powder room, two offices and a couple of closed doors. At the very end, we stopped in front of an elevator. Francesca turned, and gave us a dazzling smile. Her eyes looked like bright blue bullets.

"Elevator!" she announced, with a sweep of her arm.

"Great! Let's take a ride," Paul said. The three of us in the elevator made for a tight squeeze. Francesca flattened against her wall, although that did little to disguise the fact that there were really five of us crammed into that tiny elevator---me, Paul, Francesca, and her per-son-al-i-ty.

"This is kind of tight for a catering operation," Paul observed while holding his breath.

"This is a private residence, not the Waldorf Astoria," Francesca snapped. "They have to make several trips."

One floor down the elevator opened onto a narrow hall lined with doors and with a ceiling so low I could touch the pipes and air shafts overhead. Francesca stepped out, pulled a tight 180 and led us out the back door at the north end of the house. We were standing in a parking lot for perhaps six cars, shielded from the front of the house by ten-foot yews and hollies.

"Voilà!" roared Francesca. "I give you the service entrance! The vans park here. They bring trolleys. The food is in pots, bowls, roasting pans. They wheel it in; it goes upstairs. The wait staff comes in, sets up the tables, the bars, organizes the canapés. They begin early that morning and are sometimes here all day depending on the size of the party. The food is the last thing to arrive."

"And do you supervise all this?" Paul asked. I felt sorry for him.

"Are you out of your mind?" Francesca hissed, in a tone reserved for people who ask if Lilibet polishes her own crowns. "We have a major domo, Big Ben. Lindsey has met him 200 times, he's always here to help run a big party, he's 6'9", very hard to miss him. He supervises the caterers. Certainly I look in from time to time myself but by the time the napkins are folded and the glasses set out, the work is finished. That's why one hires a first-class operation in the first place, to make sure every detail is correct."

"How would you say the evening went?" Paul asked.

"One of the reasons I often use the Culinary Institute is their reliability. It's an exceptional training facility for the culinary sciences---and a hell of a lot cheaper than Le Boeuf from the city, although we do use them from time to time."

She smiled faux-sweetly. "What else can I tell you? And what the hell is so important about the food? Why would you think something she ate gave her a heart attack? I repeat," she bellowed angrily, "no one else who dined here dropped dead!"

"Let's go over the menu and the seating chart," said Paul the Stoic.

We got back into the elevator which seemed smaller still, filled as it now was with Francesca's steam. Upstairs, we followed Francesca into her office. She pulled some papers out of a drawer and shoved them at Paul.

"Here's the seating chart. Here's the damned menu with my notes to the chef. First course was local smoked sturgeon tossed with shaved ginger on a bed of local greens. Second course---you know, you both were here and ate this food!"---Francesca's patience was almost gone---"so do let me know if I skip anything, was mustard and herb crusted lamb chops. Peas with mint and shallots. Third course---dessert buffet. Coffee and tea served at table. Chocolates. Anything else?"

"What about wines?"

"Waiters pour the first glass, then the bottles are left on the table."

"Place cards, as usual?" I asked.

"Of course place cards," Francesca snapped. "Everyone is put in a particular chair for a reason."

"Why was Lindsey invited?" Paul asked.

"She's a reasonably attractive woman and she can be quite amusing. *In the past,*" she emphasized, "I have relied on her to help me cultivate new donors." Francesca smiled. I smiled but I made a mental note. If the dynamic was changing, apparently had already changed, perhaps I'd better add some English of my own. I'm not Betty's daughter for nothing.

"So," I opined, "with place cards, a particular plate could have been delivered to a particular person, no?"

"Absolutely," Francesca replied crisply. "Someone always has a special plate. Florence Fein keeps kosher, Jill Morris is a vegan, and Kathy Hanover has to have fish."

"Did you have the usual staff from the CIA?" I asked.

"There is no usual staff. They rotate servers, sous chefs. Usually we are assigned one master chef for the season but that night our regular man was replaced by another chef. Working our parties is a big deal and he probably pulled rank."

Paul said, "Mrs. O'Connell, thank you for being so helpful. I think that is all for now. Is your husband here?"

"Not now. He went to New York this morning. He'll be back later this afternoon. Then he'll be at the pool."

Paul said, "Fine. We'll catch up with him there."

As Paul and I stood, Francesca said, "Lindsey, I'd like a private word with you."

Paul said, "You ladies go ahead. Lindsey, I'll be on the porch."

I followed Francesca into her office. She closed the door behind us and hissed, "Just between us girls, what is the problem here?"

"Francesca, you know that when someone dies, questions have to be asked."

"The bitch had a heart attack. Do you realize what this could do to our reputations, to say nothing of Franklin's business if it got out that she died as a result of something she ate at one of my parties? I guess I was wrong about you. You seemed smart but you don't have a clue, do you?"

"The fact is that Cassandra died suddenly and we are trying to piece together the reason why."

"You saw her! She had a frigging heart attack or a stroke. This is the most offensive thing that has ever happened to me. And the rudest."

"Initially it appeared that she had a heart attack but the preliminary autopsy results indicate there may have been another issue. Something she ate."

"Like what?" Francesca demanded.

"Francesca, I'm so sorry, but that is all I can say for now."

"It is clear to me our friendship has meant nothing to you. Such a betrayal! I value loyalty above all." Her lips were twitching in a frightening way and I wondered if she were about to strike me.

As I walked outside to meet Paul, the bright sunshine seemed exponentially warmer after the icy anger. My stomach churned. I loathe confrontations. Was Francesca trying to hide something?

I'd never been on the receiving end of a hate laser but I didn't like it.

And no, I didn't have a clue. But I planned on getting one.

Paul interrupted my fretting.

"Come on, Lindsey. Time to go see the cooks."

A Visit to the CIA

When you are headed down Route 9 out of Rhinebeck, the first thing that happens is Staatsburg. On the right, you will glimpse the Mills Mansion with its two hundred acres of rolling, wooded grounds beside the River.

The existing house is the third to stand on the site. A 25-room Greek revival structure built in 1832 by Morgan Lewis and his wife, Gertrude Livingston, replaced an earlier house that had burned down. This second house was inherited by Ruth Livingston Mills, wife of noted financier and philanthropist Ogden Mills.

In 1895, Mr. and Mrs. Mills commissioned the prestigious New York City architectural firm of McKim, Mead and White to drastically remodel and, within a year, the house was transformed into a Beaux-Arts mansion of 65 rooms and 14 bathrooms, its exterior embellished with balustrades, pilasters, floral swags, and a massive portico. The rooms were furnished with elaborately carved and gilded furniture, fine oriental rugs, silk fabrics, and a collection of art objects from Europe, ancient Greece, and the Far East. The entire effect is sumptuous and rivals some of the Newport cottages in opulence. If you haven't visited, come in the spring, tour the house, and then have your picnic basket on the lawn. The River views are sublime.

Then we have Hyde Park, the Beaux-Arts gem for whom the hamlet is named. One of the country homes of Frederick and Louise Vanderbilt, Hyde Park is another fine example of estates built by tycoons in the Gilded Age. The architecture and Parmentier's landscaping are superb. Interestingly, the furnishings and decorations cost twice as much as the house itself but the effect, I am sad to say, has always seemed to me to resemble my notion of a first class 19th century Parisian bordello. 'Thank God for the Vanderbilts,' a society columnist wrote after attending the opening of the house. 'They can always be relied upon in times of dullness to furnish a sensation of some kind.'

Then we come to Springwood, FDR's home, with its spacious front lawn and tree-lined drive, as well as his museum and visitors' center, and lovely meadows surrounding the President's and Eleanor's graves, and that of his Scottish terrier, Fala. There's the FDR Drive-in Movie and Liquorama where Huxley buys all his booze. Most of the area is small town stuff, with small strip malls, small carpet stores, and small white frame houses too close to the traffic since the road was widened in the late 60s. Just your average small town.

Until, that is, you reach the Culinary Institute of America, arguably the world's greatest culinary college, whose graduates run many of the finest kitchens and restaurants on earth.

The CIA, as it is known, is a large complex stretching over seventy hilly, wooded acres stretching from Route 9 down to the east bank of the Hudson River. Most of the handsome buildings are several stories of red brick with white shutters, dormers, and colonial facades. Three restaurants---French, Italian, and American farm-to-table cuisines---are situated at the base of the hills. Almost three thousand students and a couple of hundred faculty are housed there as they devote themselves to perfecting the culinary arts.

In addition to being world-renowned, with branches in Napa and St. Helena, San Antonio, and Singapore, the CIA's mother ship is a tremendous resource for local party-givers who are fortunate enough to live in the Hudson River Valley. Students serve as sous-chefs and waiters; seniors, graduate students, and faculty serve as chefs. Having the CIA cater a party costs less than hiring a top New York restaurant, the staff is well-trained, and the food is imaginative and superb.

In the reception area, we were met by Ray Winship, one of the CIA's managing directors, a shortish man of about fifty, natty in a navy blazer over a crisp blue cambric shirt with cufflinks and a red knit tie over gray slacks and black Gucci loafers. He wore black glasses with round frames and had short, black, close-cropped hair.

Shaking hands with Paul and me, Winship said, "You're here about the O'Connell party. Let me walk you through the process."

Leading us down several corridors, he said, "The O'Connell party began here."

We entered an hotel-size kitchen. Long steel tables stood in the center of the room above which were suspended every shape and type of pot, pan, roaster, basket, strainer, and colander known to man. Triple sinks, triple dishwashers, and rolling sheet pan racks stood alongside glass-fronted refrigerators and freezers. Butcher-block counters stood against three walls and above them magnetic strips held knives, cleavers, spoons, whisks, skewers, spatulas and other implements of every size and description. Large mixers, blenders, microwaves, and food processors stood at attention below a long wall of shelving holding casseroles, bowls, tureens, platters, charlottes, and molds. Until the rise of the Food Network, most of us had never been behind the scenes in a commercial food service facility. Paul and I gaped at the diversity and range of the array and I made a mental note to buy a new oven mitt.

"This is where the food for Francesca O'Connell's party was prepared that day, in Master Kitchen A, one of three master kitchens used for events we are catering. Through those doors are two prep kitchens that serve this master."

"You have an entire kitchen for prep?" Paul asked.

"Oh, yes. We do so much mincing and dicing," said Mr. Winship, with a twinkle.

"Outside here," and we stepped out and across a hall, "we have several classrooms where menus, timing, and cooking techniques are discussed."

The room was equipped with several computer stations, AV equipment, and posters showing various concoctions---a crêpe suzette flaming, a timbale garnished with crustaceans, an artichoke gratineé with steam rising above its golden crust.

Paul said, "We going to need to talk to everyone who worked that party. How quickly can they be pulled together?"

Mr. Winship looked at his watch, then consulted several sheets of paper on his clipboard, consulted his watch again, then turned to us and said, "Team Béchamel is up to their elbows in barquettes right this minute. They're just down the hall."

"Team Béchamel? I beg your pardon?" I didn't understand and Paul had screwed up his face.

Winship said, "Each semester we divide the students doing their practicums into crews. We give the crews names. This year, they're sauces. Béchamel, Mornay, Hollandaise, Newberg, and Rémoulade. Last year they were lettuces."

"Ahhhh! How clever!" I said. "And you say they're...where just now?"

"Right this way!" and taking Paul and me by our elbows, Mr. Winship lead us out. Down a corridor and a turn to the left later we found ourselves in a smaller kitchen/classroom where a dozen or so young men and women worked on a single long marble table top. Before them were piles of phyllo pastry and miniature tart pans.

The instructor intoned, "Keep it light! Keep it up! Fingertips! Fingertips! Gently up! Gently out! That's it! That's it! And into the little boats!"

At our arrival the instructor stopped, threw up his hands and cried, "Look, class! A surprise inspection! Management on the floor!"

Mr. Winship and his clipboard strode to the front of the class.

"André, may I present Mr. Paul Whitbeck and Ms. Lindsey Brooks. They are here to accumulate information about the O'Connells' party. We must give them our attention and our entire cooperation. I suggest we take our seats."

Standing in front of the group, Paul began, "How did you prep for the party that evening? Tell us every step from A to Z."

A woman spoke first.

"The two of us who are team captains, myself, I'm Michele, and Malcolm,"---she pointed to a fellow who raised his hand in acknowledgement---"and our supervisor, Perry, went to meet with Mrs. O'Connell at her house a few weeks ago. We brought menus with us so she could see our seasonal specials and standard dishes."

"Is Perry here?" Paul asked, scanning the class.

"No," Malcolm spoke up. "Perry is missing in action."

"What does that mean?" Paul asked.

Winship interjected, "I beg your pardon? Missing in action?"

Michele answered "Perry went with us to the house earlier in the day of the party to get the set-ups started, then came back here and supervised the cooking, then rode over with the food in the delivery vans. As we were about to begin serving, another chef arrived to say Perry had become unwell. Apparently Perry called the office and asked to have a substitute sent over."

"And who was that?" Paul asked.

"None of us knew him," Michelle answered, "but we don't know everyone on the faculty. We just figured it had been pretty much whoever they could get, being that it was such short notice. At that point it didn't make much difference because we all knew what to do anyway. On the day of an event, the supervisors do just that---supervise our doing what they have already trained us to do."

"So you're saying a person you didn't know appeared at the O'Connells'?" I asked. The girl nodded.

"And supervised the last stage of food prep?" She nodded.

I turned to Mr. Winship and André.

"Who was your replacement for Perry?"

Mr. Winship looked very worried. Shaking his head, he said, "No one called that night about being ill. And we sent no replacement. This is the first I've heard of this."

Paul asked, "How many of your people went?"

The woman answered, "Twelve."

I spoke up, "And the eleven of you who were there are here right now? No one else worked the party?"

"That's right."

We left the students sitting where they were and asked Mr. Winship and André to step into another room.

Paul said, "We are going to have to question each of these students."

Winship and André nodded gravely.

"I'll be sending two officers over this afternoon. Make sure none of these students leaves the campus."

"You're sure you haven't heard anything from this guy Perry?" Paul asked.

"No. And that is most unusual. I had no idea he was…well, *missing*."

"Do you have a photograph of Perry?" I asked.

"We do, we have photos of all faculty. Look," and Mr. Winship stepped over to a desk. A few taps on the computer brought up a page showing a blonde, smiling man in a chef's toque.

"This is Perry Burr," said Mr. Winship. "The chef for the O'Connells' party."

Franklin's Secrets and the Boathouse

After the CIA, we headed back to the O'Connells' to see Franklin. Getting out of the car and heading around the house to the pool, I remarked, "Well, this case will mark the end of my beautiful friendship with the O'Connells."

"That Francesca is a piece of work," Paul grumbled. "I thought you were really good friends. How can she be angry with you for helping me out on a murder investigation? Oh, wait! Other than the fact she's shaping up to be our prime suspect."

That may have sounded light but Paul was speaking in his bulldog voice.

"With Francesca, you're friends until things change, I guess." Or until you're helping run a criminal investigation.

We turned the corner around the shrubbery when Paul suddenly stopped and pointed up, "Well, lookee there!" A video camera was perched on the side of the house. "Damn! We should have sussed that out earlier," he said. "I'm going to go requisition the footage from the night of the party," he said. "Meet you at the pool."

I continued down to the cabana, a small post-modern building of local stone Franklin had built beside his infinity pool. The bottom of the pool was a mosaic of the three fates, the Moirae, Greek deities who manage the threads of destiny that control our lives. Clotho, who spins the Thread of Life; Lachesis, who allots the length of the yarn; and Atropos, who cuts the thread.

Franklin, deeply tanned and wearing black trunks and a khaki t-shirt, lay on a chaise beside the pool looking at the mountains and the river. I said hello, Franklin nodded.

"Sit," he said. I sat on a chaise next to him for several minutes with neither of us saying anything.

"You're quiet, Franklin," I ventured.

"Just when you start thinking life is good, something happens and it doesn't seem so good." I couldn't see his eyes beneath his Ray-Bans.

"Murders do tend to put one off one's feed."

"It isn't funny, Lindsey."

"I know it isn't, Franklin. I'm sorry."

"When you get to be my age, people start disappearing. Just when I get comfortable, somebody pops off. You never know. I could be next."

"Franklin, don't be silly. You look great."

"I'm old."

I answered, "Franklin, you are certainly not old. You are a man at the top of his game. Brain fast as lightning and the body of a thirty-year-old."

"That's what she said."

"Who said?"

"Cassandra."

I sighed and thought, "Oh hell, here comes the motive."

Aloud, I said, "Well, anyone would say that, the way you prance around in those tight little Missoni tops Francesca buys for you. Franklin, you're as healthy as a horse. You have a trainer three times a week, you jog, and you give teenagers a run for their money on the tennis court. You drive race cars. You'll probably live to be 400. We should start calling you Methuselah." I gave him an adoring smile but Franklin was having none of it.

"What's that poem? 'Twenty-two roads diverged in a yellow wood'---and I only had time to take half of them."

I smiled. "What roads did you miss, Franklin? You have a beautiful wife..."

"She's bored with me."

"...a beautiful son..."

105

"He only cares about the money."

"...a wonderful business..."

"After the first few billions, it's old hat."

"...your philanthropy makes a difference..."

"Every battle's a losing battle."

"All right, you tell me what's missing," I suggested.

"I'd like to be in love again. Like the first time."

We sat quietly for a few moments. Then he continued, "We met when I was a stage door Johnnie. Never thought she'd look at me, couldn't believe I did it. I stood there on 45th Street waiting for her to come out after a performance and gave her a bouquet of daisies. How corny is that? We saw each other constantly until I shipped out. How corny is *that*. I said to her, 'Well, honey---we'll always have Pelham Bay Park.' "

"Have where?" I asked.

Franklin said impatiently, "You *know*, like from *Casablanca*. She and I never had Paris like Bogie and his girl. We just had a woodsy little clearing in the Bronx on Mondays when her show was dark. Back then Pelham Bay was the country. There was a hill where you could have a picnic and look out at the Sound."

Suddenly Big Ben and a groundskeeper came running toward us.

"Mr. O'Connell!" he shouted. "Mr. O'Connell! I need to talk to you, sir."

"Yes, Ben. What is it?" Franklin sighed and turned to him, squinting against the sun.

Ben hesitated.

"Come on, man!" Franklin snapped.

"Sir, there's a dead body in the boathouse."

"My Christ!" said Franklin O'Connell.

♦♦♦♦♦

An hour later, as several policemen moved about the grounds, Paul returned to where Franklin and I sat on a stone wall.

"Given the chef's coat, I would say we may have found that guy Perry who's missing from the CIA," he said.

"What happened?" I asked.

"Somebody brained him, apparently with the boat gaff that has blood all over the end. The poor soul has been there zipped inside a rigging bag since Saturday. That's why no one noticed anything until now. The body was sealed up. My guys are still down there but I've sent the body over to the examiner."

♦♦♦♦♦

Paul called the CIA and got Winship on the phone.

"Have you heard anything from Perry?" Paul asked.

"I have not," replied Mr. Winship gravely. "We are all so worried."

Paul said, "I'm afraid that we're going to have to ask you to identify a body. Someone was killed the night of the party. It could be your man Perry."

I arrived home to find Bennett in the kitchen garnishing a pile of shrimp.

I leaned my head on his shoulder and sighed.

"Are we weary?" he inquired.

"I'm depressed. Come sit down and comfort me."

"I fly to your side, Madame," said Bennett, hastily drying his hands and grabbing two glasses from the freezer. "It's that magical hour of the evening, Madame," he said. "Everything is on the porch."

We settled ourselves in our customary chairs. The western sky had wide swaths of clouds promising a beautiful sunset. Bennett expertly agitated the martini shaker and poured two cold vodkas, then sprinkled them with lemon twist spirals.

"What have we learned?" he asked, taking the chair beside me.

"Initially, as you know, Cassandra's death appeared to have been a straightforward heart attack. She had seen a cardiologist when she arrived here six weeks ago. Had a history of arrhythmia. There didn't appear to be anything suspicious but the autopsy proved otherwise."

"I'm glad you persuaded him to order an autopsy. And it revealed the cause of death to be...??"

"Poison."

"What?" Bennett sat up and put his glass down. "You aren't serious!"

"Poison," I nodded. "Aconite. Do you remember the first course that night? It was smoked fish with several ground-up things on top --- raw vegetables, nuts, ginger, and fruits. My guess is that the Monk's Hood was grated on the particular salad Cassandra was served, along with the shaved ginger and nuts and the rest of it. All the killer had to do was to check the place cards and make sure the right salad, the one with the aconite, got to the right place."

Bennett pondered. "Of course, it could also have been disguised as some part of the main course. Aconite-encrusted lamb chops, aconite gratineé, aconite-infused pommes de terre. How much poison are we talking about?"

"According to Carver, the coroner---

"---the coroner's name is 'Carver?' Grim."

"---according to Carver, two tablespoons would have done it."

"Oh, dear."

"It also turns out the CIA chef who worked the party that night vanished."

"Oh, dear."

"Late this afternoon we found a body in the boathouse at the O'Connells'."

"Oh, dear."

"The body in the boathouse was the missing CIA chef sent to do the party at the O'Connells'."

"Crikey!" Bennett cried. "Talk about the wrong place at the wrong time! Egads!"

We sat quietly, gratefully sipping our vodkas.

After a few moments, Bennett said, "Then again, we have no reason to be sure that Cassandra was the intended victim at all, do we?"

"We don't?" I said.

"Couldn't the poison have been on any random canapé? That would seem to be a surer thing---little morsels popped into one's mouth whole?"

"A random killing. It is something to consider, I suppose. Makes things even more complicated. What would that achieve?"

"Notoriety for the O'Connells. Extremely bad press for Franklin's public profile, his companies. I hear he has some largish deals coming along."

"True. However, if we assume Cassandra *was* the target, it could also point to Francesca because the fatal dinner took place at her house."

"Francesca? But what would have been her motive?"

"She may have figured out that Cassandra had more than a passing interest in Franklin."

Bennett scoffed. "Franklin? Don't be ridiculous. Cassandra was the type of woman who flirted with everyone, even a humble butler! I certainly noticed her blandishments toward Franklin but I can't believe Francesca would have taken them seriously---or would have thought Franklin reciprocated any affection. He's devoted to Francesca."

"Franklin and Cassandra were lovers some years ago before he met and married Francesca."

Bennett bared his teeth in a grimace. "Ouch, madame. And Francesca is aware of their former relationship?"

"I honestly don't know. I once asked Francesca what she would do to anyone who made a play for Franklin."

"And her answer?"

"Piano wire."

Bennett gestured to the porch sideboard. "Madame, you are aware that those pieces have nothing to do with each other?"

He was referring to several juleps clustered on a tray surrounding a small ice bucket.

"Nothing to do with each other? How do you mean?"

"They are clustered together, yes. They are all silver. But the cups are from five different manufacturers. Their styles are similar, but not identical. The salver is in the style of George III but in fact was cast in 1900. The ice bucket is from Peru and is late Colonial."

"And your point is?"

"Perhaps the deaths appear to be connected and have certain things in common---timing, proximity, location---but, in reality, have nothing to do with each other. The missing chef puts the spotlight on whoever killed him---or is perhaps only a distraction? What does the CIA have to say about all this? And you *haven't* asked Francesca if she knew about Cassandra's interest in her husband? If she knew they had been lovers?"

"To repeat, why the hell would I have that conversation?"

"Well," Bennett replied, "someone has to have it. And someone has to ask Franklin why he invited Cassandra to Rhinebeck in the first place."

"You don't think Franklin is a suspect?" I asked.

"And didn't Cassandra's late husband have children?"

"His aren't the only children we need to know about. Apparently Cassandra might have had one of her own."

"You don't say! Any thoughts on paternity? Or the little one's whereabouts now?" Bennett asked.

"That's for tomorrow." Jiggling my glass, I asked, "May I have a dividend?"

Strolling with our drinks on the porch, I said, "Not that we knew a poisoning was afoot but I do wish I had paid more attention to the plating that night."

"Perhaps I can help you with that for the first course."

"How's that?" I asked as Bennett retrieved his phone from his jacket pocket.

"Where is it? Where is it?" Bennett murmured as he swiped the screen. "Yes! Here it is, madame." And on his phone was a photograph of the table where we had been seated with the pre-set salads in place.

"I can't believe you have this! Why did you take it?"

"I thought the centerpieces were especially lovely. I took the picture as a reference for the still life I planned to paint."

"I think Paul can get this analyzed to show the aconite. Nice work, Bennett!"

RESEARCH IN TIVOLI

Paul and I drove over to the Madalin for a cup of coffee. Joe, the owner, was settled at a table on the porch riffling through notes on index cards.

"What's up, Jose?" I asked.

"I'm just going over menus," he answered. "Do you think people still care about crab cakes---or should we take them off?"

"I live for them!" I said. "And yours are very good. Right up there with the Harvard Club."

"The Harvard Club chef has a secret ingredient. He puts ivy in them," Joe smirked. "What can I get you? You guys want a cup of coffee? A beer? Have you had lunch?"

Paul said, "We came for coffee and to ask you a few questions if you've got a minute." Joe gestured for us to sit and waved over a waiter. "Although I wouldn't mind splitting a club sandwich if Lindsey is agreeable."

"You don't have to share anything, you're my guests."

"No, thanks, I'm watching my trim and girlish figure," Paul smiled. "Lindsey gave me a lecture about portion control. So when she's watching, I portion out my control over my fork."

Our order duly taken, Paul began, "Was Cassandra Chappelle a regular here?"

Joe replied, "Everyone is a regular here, Sheriff. If you are drawing breath within thirty miles, you're a regular. Location, location, location. Sure, she came here a lot."

"Who was she with?" I asked.

"She'd come in with Huxley. The Strattons who own Twin Pines. A lot of folks. Who are you looking for?"

"Doctor Vance."

Joe nodded. "Plenty of times."

"How did they behave?" I asked.

"Kind of like they were on a date. Not that they held hands or anything but they clearly enjoyed each other's company a good deal."

Paul and I looked at each other.

"But," Joe continued, "the lady played the field. She had a lot of date nights."

"With whom?" I asked.

"Do you know Don Palmer? He teaches at Bard. He's a regular here and they came in a few times for dinner. She also came in with some students I gather she'd been coaching, one guy in particular, I think his name was Brad." He stopped. "Wasn't that the kid who died? Yikes! She came in with him and maybe his girlfriend a time or two, took them to dinner. Then after a while just she and he came in for dinner. A lot."

"Did that look like a 'date night'?" Paul asked.

"I'd say so," nodded Joe.

Paul and I looked at each other.

"I'll tell you something else. They also spent time looking at papers, documents or something. Hey! I keep my eyes open around here. Don't forget, I was a lawyer before I started slinging hash." He paused. "I mean, creating culinary delights."

We headed back over to the Bard office.

I drove while Paul barked orders into the phone.

"I want to know if any of the CIA students took any classes at Bard, had any friends at Bard, relatives at Bard, either students or faculty. Did they know Cassandra Chappelle? Did they know Brad Ruffin? Did they know the O'Connells other than working that party? And I want to know where each of them is from, how long they've been here, where they were before, what they do in their spare time. We are looking for a connection. I want to know why they chose to come here to school and who their friends are. Check to see if anybody has a record. Find out if they noticed anything unusual the night of the party. I want all this done in the next two days."

As we turned into the Bard campus, I said, "Hearing what we just heard about Palmer, Cassandra, and Brad gives us new leads we didn't have before. That's a break in the case, right?"

"I'm not sure if it's a break or a complication. Never judge a gift horse by its cover."

Paul arranged for Francesca to come to the incident room at Bard.

The sight of Mrs. Franklin O'Connell arriving in a cloud of White Shoulders and ivory linen was the most extraordinary thing the sergeants had ever seen. They leaped to their feet and scrambled to offer her a chair.

Francesca took a seat. Paul stood and began pointing out various photographs and timelines which were tacked up across 4 by 8' corkboards across all four walls of the room.

"This is where we are, Mrs. O'Connell. Cassandra Chappelle had dinner at your house on July 20. About an hour later, she succumbed to poisoning. The autopsy examination of her stomach contents found a fatal amount of aconite mingled with the lamb and other food she ate at your house earlier that evening."

"I fail to see what that has to do with me."

Paul's eyebrows shot up. He leaned into Francesca's face and snapped, "Well, lady, you're the only one who is not making any connection. The food she ate was ordered by you, prepared in your kitchen, and served to people in assigned seats at your house."

"Choosing a menu makes me the hostess, not necessarily the murderer. You haven't one iota of proof of my involvement in any of this."

"The supervisor from the CIA is mysteriously replaced by we don't know who and the real chef turns up dead in your boathouse."

115

"Are you suggesting I left the party, dragging the chef behind me, then lured him to the boathouse, killed him, then hired some thug as a substitute? Clearly, you've never run a party for two hundred people. Speaking of which, you were there that night! You saw me! I was in front of everyone all the time, every minute."

"Not every minute. Are you telling me you never went into the kitchen?"

"Of course, I went to the kitchen. The chef had to get approval on plating, among other things. And there's always some issue, they can't find the ice shaver, can't remember who gets the vegetarian plate, the kosher plate, the…"

"Those are special plates that go to particular places?"

"For the tenth time, yes. Certainly. If you will review the instructions I sent the CIA, you will see that all is specified and, as Lindsey can tell you, that goes on at every party. Besides, that isn't the point, is it? In order for me to do what you are saying, you'd have to get corroboration from the chef."

"But he's dead."

"I could not possibly have killed him. Look at me! I'm not the kind of woman who can overpower a man. I'm no karate expert! I don't even do Pilates!"

"But you have a staff---we'll want to talk to your major domo."

♦ ♦ ♦ ♦ ♦

Benjamin Barrow---Big Ben---ran the operation of the O'Connells' estate.

Ben stood about 6'9" and must have weighed in at 300 or so, mostly muscle.

When he stood next to Paul, the sheriff looked like a bantam rooster.

To take the edge off their size differential, Paul put Barrow in a lowish chair while he perched directly in front of him on a tall stool.

"Where you from, Mr. Barrow?" Paul asked.

"Down the road."

"Down the road where?"

"Just below Rhinecliff."

"What did your father work at?"

"My dad worked on estates. Wilderstein, Wildercliff, Springfield. Sometimes others."

"Doing what?"

"Maintain the grounds. Mother cooked and cleaned. Fill in stuff, mostly."

"You ever help your dad? Work in the summers, after school, that kind of thing?"

He nodded. "All the time."

"I see now why the O'Connells' place looks so good. You grew up learning how to take care of an estate. How long have you worked for the O'Connells?" Paul asked.

"Since they came here, about fifteen years."

"What do you do for them?"

"I run the yard crews, manage the maintenance, and look after anything else that needs to be done, supervising hired hands, catering and otherwise who come onto the property to perform whatever services."

"Lot of machinery to look after?"

Barrow nodded. "It takes a lot of equipment to keep this place looking right. I like to do things before the O'Connells have to ask me to. Like the stone walls, keep them in good order. Shrubbery, keep that trimmed. Keep the painting up. Keep his cars washed and polished. Mr. O'Connell wants everything just so."

"What about Mrs. O'Connell?"

"Her, too. She likes what she likes and she likes it right when she wants it."

"Ever have any trouble around here?'

"What kind of trouble?"

"People trespassing, that sort of thing."

"Not as a rule. There's a stone wall around the whole place. There's closed circuit cameras, I got an ex-cop who just watches those. Motion detectors, too. Most of the time the main gate is closed. Guests know to come in the farm gate. But that's usually closed, and they have to be buzzed in, unless Mr. and Mrs. are having a few people over. Big party like the one you're asking about, main gate is open."

"Any security there?"

He shook his head. "Not as a rule. Slows things up."

I interjected, "There's almost never a guest list at the gate."

"Then how the hell do you keep Jane Q. Doe or John Q. Public from just dropping in?" Paul demanded with evident incredulity.

Barrow shrugged. "Somebody comes who don't belong gets noticed quick."

Paul was not happy with that explanation or the lack of security.

"Take us through what you did the night of the party," he snapped.

"Got here early and helped set up the tables and chairs in the ballroom according to Mrs. O'Connell's chart. Watched for the caterers to arrive. Made sure they parked right and didn't bang up the place bringing in their equipment. Made sure everything was unloaded and set up, made sure all the tables got fixed with the tablecloths and knives and forks, helped the florists unload, then went home and changed into a suit and tie and came back. Walked around, moved through all the rooms, watched what went on, kept an eye on Mrs. O'Connell to see what else she needed spur of the moment, like. After the people left, I supervised it all in reverse. Got the caterers out the door, got the tables broken down and hauled away to the barns where they get stored along with the chairs."

"Everything go according to plan?"

"Seemed to me it did."

"Were you aware the supervisor from the CIA was replaced?"

"Hell, that wasn't anything I would have noticed. All those people look pretty much the same to me. Hardly a week goes by that we don't have some sort of event here, whether it's a dinner or a cocktail party or a benefit or something. Sometimes she gets people from the city to come up and do it, sometimes a restaurant in the Village, sometimes the CIA. I don't keep 'em all straight, how could I?"

"Then how can you ensure the O'Connells' security?"

"I take care of things. Nothing's happened to them yet."

FOOTAGE FROM THE O'CONNELLS

With Paul clutching the CIA's photograph of the dead chef Perry, I joined him and his two deputies upstairs in our office at Bard screening the O'Connells' security camera tape. In the middle of the afternoon, a shout came from Sgt. O'Reilly.

"Look at this!" The deputy rewound the tape. "It's grainy as hell but I think this is your guy." The tape showed Perry arriving and supervising the unloading of food from a van. "Now we fast forward to about an hour or so later, and we see him coming back outside. He walks to the edge of the camera range, and fires up a cigarette." The figure stood smoking, then looked over and began to talk to someone off-camera. Then he exited stage right.

Paul said, "That's the CIA guy. Does he come back?"

His officer said, "He doesn't, but about ten minutes later"---he advanced the tape again---"this guy comes back. He's putting on a chef's hat."

"He's a good bit taller. He's got a beard. But his face is blurred. He must have been running. Take this over there and get Winship to look at it," Paul said.

Paul's officer drove over and screened the tape for Winship and the students who had worked the party that night. None of them knew who the man was even though they had worked with him that evening and the tape was so grainy they couldn't even make a definite ID.

Paul was not heartened by the news. "How the hell can they work with the guy and not be able to describe him?"

Paul's officer answered, "Winship said, 'This man had a mustache and beard? That should have given him away! The CIA doesn't allow facial hair.' I guess the kids might not have thought about that."

I said, "So it was some guy in a disguise. He came in posing as CIA faculty, conked the actual chef, doctored the salad, put it at Cassandra's place himself, then left."

"Well," Paul said, "that's one way to look at it."

"What's your way?" I asked.

Paul gestured to the deputies, two nice-looking young men maybe thirty years old.

"Lindsey, you been working around these boys for the last few days but let me make official introductions. Meet Sgt. Wingate Jackson and Sgt. Edwin O'Reilly. These are two of Rhinebeck's finest. Tell Miss Brooks what you lads have sussed out here."

"First things are motive, means, and opportunity. We only see one person who has all of these."

"And who might that be?" I asked.

"Francesca O'Connell," replied the deputies.

"Don't be absurd," I muttered. "She has too much to lose."

"Isn't that the motive, though, Lindsey? She was worried about losing her husband?" I hate it when Paul arches his damned eyebrows like that.

"Go ahead." Paul nodded to the two men.

Standing, and holding a ruler as he walked over to a display of photos of Francesca and a timeline, Jackson began.

Pointing to an enlargement of Bennett's photo of the pre-set salads served to our table that evening, he said, "Notice the little shavings on top. On every salad but one, these were only shaved ginger. On one salad---the salad delivered specifically to the deceased, Cassandra Chappelle---the ginger was combined with at least two tablespoons of shaved aconite root and shredded aconite leaves. The ginger would have masked the taste."

He turned to me. "Miss Brooks, I think you told the Sheriff that you knew Mrs. O'Connell had aconite on her property, that you had personally given her plants for her garden. Is that correct?"

I nodded.

He then pointed to a photo of the O'Connells taken the night of the party. They were obviously having an argument. Franklin gripped Francesca's upper arm tightly, Francesca's face was contorted in rage.

"The photographer at the dinner took this, er, candid shot. Most people would say the O'Connells are happily married but this shows a big argument. We also have witnesses who say they had a screamfest behind the door of the library that night. We also have statements from people who sat at Mrs. O'Connells' table who quoted her as saying, 'That bitch. I'd like to kill her,' spoken when her husband was escorting the deceased around. These witnesses also said Mr. O'Connell spent all his time that evening with the deceased."

He continued. "Far from being in plain sight all night, Mrs. O'Connell was in and out of the kitchen. It would have been a simple matter for her to put the poison on a salad and to then have instructed a server to put that particular salad at the deceased's place at the correct table.

"We also have this bit of evidence recovered from the deceased's house."

He held up the 'slow boat to China' envelope Cassandra had shown me.

"According to Miss Chappelle's housekeeper, this arrived in the mail several days before the event. She remembered it because the envelope had no return address. This ticket was enclosed. It is a one-way booking aboard a Seabourne ship from New York to Shanghai. The issuing travel agent is in Poughkeepsie; she said a very tall man paid for it in cash. We showed her a photograph of the O'Connells' farm manager, Ben

Barrow. She confirmed that he was the purchaser. In addition, Mrs. O'Connell's fingerprints are on both the letter and the ticket."

I could see where this was going. Did not look good.

"The sheriff has some additional points to add."

Paul stood and walked over to some old headshots of Cassandra from her *Harlot* days as well as a couple of candids from the night of the party.

"She was a beautiful woman. Mr. O'Connell knew her in her Broadway days and has admitted they had an affair. We think he was planning to leave his wife and marry Cassandra. He spoke of her in very tender terms just two days ago."

"What do you say, Lindsey?"

"Oh, come on, Paul. It's all circumstantial. How do you explain the CIA chef in the boathouse? What did he have to do with this 'plot' you think you see?"

"Look at it this way, Lindsey. Suppose the chef saw Mrs. O'Connell tampering with a salad and asked her what she was doing. It would have been a simple matter to have Barrow take him away."

"OK, suppose he did ask Francesca what she was doing. Hell, she didn't have to have the poor man killed, she could have just told him to mind his own business, told him she was making something special for a special guest."

"Not if she worried about having him be a witness after Chappelle turned up dead," observed Sergeant O'Reilly astutely.

"What about the substitute chef we saw on the surveillance tape?" I asked.

"That could very well be Big Ben. That man is a good half foot taller than the actual CIA chef."

Paul frowned. "I know she is---or used to be---a friend of yours, Lindsey. But look at the facts. She had a lot to lose if Franklin decided to make a change."

I just sat. Very bad. Very bad.

"Lindsey, you and I have to go to the boathouse autopsy. That may answer some questions.

"In the meantime, you boys get that guy Big Ben back in here at 4 o'clock."

Autopsy of Body in Boathouse

"Hello, again, Dr. Carver," I said.

"Hello, again, Lindsey, Sheriff. Why don't you step over here and we can look at these photographs. I don't think you're going to want to see the body itself. The photos are bad enough."

We walked over to a stainless autopsy table where Carver laid out several 8 x 10 color photographs. He was right; it was a ghastly set of pictures.

"Male. Forty-odd years of age. Five feet eleven. Because the decomposition was well under way---the body had been sealed up and virtually poaching for a couple of days---there is no way to be precise about the time of death. Internal organs clean. We were able to match the gash on the head to the fragments of hair and blood on the gaff you retrieved at the scene, Sheriff."

"So the cause of death was blunt trauma?" Paul asked.

Carver nodded. "Yes."

I mused aloud. "The guy was hired to do a party at the O'Connells' that night. I can't understand why he was in the boathouse."

Paul answered. "He didn't plan on going to the boathouse. He was hauled there."

"How do you know that?" I asked.

Pulling another photo from the stack, Carver gestured, "Look here. See the bruising under the arms?"

Paul nodded. "He was dragged down to the boathouse. The heel of the one shoe he still had on showed dirt and grass consistent with being dragged and we found the other shoe next to a couple of shallow ruts behind the hedge."

Carver spoke again. "There is one other thing. His sinuses are slightly singed as though he had been hit with a knock-out spray."

Paul made a face. "Knock-out spray! Like an aerosol Mickey Finn?"

Carver nodded. "Doesn't have to be an aerosol, the stuff can be a liquid in a Windex bottle. A couple of squirts and you're out cold. The stuff started showing up in Asia in the last several years. Typical case is a prostitute picks up a John, takes him home, gives him a quick spritz, relieves him of wallet, and vanishes. Or it could have been a gas, like the Russians used in Chechnya. Knock-out gas was a fictional weapon for Batman and FuManchu but real-life equivalents are available today."

Carver smiled. Paul and I frowned.

Carver continued, "I don't know the precise chemical makeup yet, we aren't equipped to do that analysis. I sent some samples out to the Feds for testing. In most cases, the stuff doesn't kill; you just wake up with a hell of a headache. Of course, this guy did not have that problem. He was just knocked out and subsequently dispatched. Permanently."

◆◆◆◆◆

Before heading back to the incident room, Paul and I walked over to Cascades on Warren Street for a cup of strong coffee and some of Bob's comforting soup for lunch.

I said, "Had to have been a man. Too much dead weight for a woman to drag. Of course, there could have been two people doing the dragging, one being a woman."

Paul observed, "No way to tell if he knew his assailant. And where the hell does the average Joe get a knock-out spray? The internet, I suppose. Like every other god-damned weapon."

"The other thing is, since the actual chef was dead in the boathouse, whoever stepped in at the dinner that night has to be the killer. Or was in cahoots with the killer."

"We know it was a man. We know he was tall. And we know he had a beard."

"No, we don't know that. The beard could have been a disguise. Probably was."

"What we also don't know is whether Francesca O'Connell recruited him as an accomplice or if he was acting on his own. Or maybe he was just another guest? But who? And why?"

He thought for a minute.

"Still, I got a hunch Big Ben is our guy. Bet you a quarter," Paul said.

Back to Big Ben

Big Ben was back in the incident room and was not happy about it.

In the five-foot-ten versus six-foot-nine confrontation, Paul got in a few early body blows.

"Let's get something straight, right now, Mr. Barrow. A woman was murdered while she ate dinner at your employers' house. You were part of that. We're just piecing the scenario together how. You are either our primary suspect---or you are an accessory. You either planted the poison or got the chef out of the way so your boss could.

"Save us some time and tell us which it is."

Big Ben shifted in his chair, leaning forward to lean on his knees.

"How the hell do you figure that?" he snarled.

"You ever work in the garden?"

"Of course, I work in the frigging garden."

"Fine. When did Mrs. O'Connell have you dig up some aconite. The day of the party? Or was it the day before?"

"Dig up what?"

"Aconite. Monk's Hood. You don't know that plant?"

"Yeah, I know what it is. Who said she told me to dig it up? And what's the difference if I dug it up or not?"

Paul handed him stills pulled from the surveillance tape. "This guy looks like you. The footage was shot after the chef running the party had disappeared."

Ben squinted at the tape.

"You saying that's me? I sure as hell can't tell. Coulda been anyone."

129

"Probably not anyone. He was wearing a chef's hat."

"Like I said, so what?"

This exchange continued for a bit longer until what had been apparent to Ben Barrow was also apparent to Paul and me; we had nothing linking him directly to the aconite and the footage was so grainy making an exact ID was impossible.

He was there, yes. He had the opportunity, yes. But the proof was going to take something more.

BACK TO THE CASE OF BRAD

Back at the incident room, Paul vented his frustration by slamming things around and swearing at random.

He said, "There are too damn many loose ends here. Let's set Cassandra aside for a moment. We don't know who killed her yet but we do know that boy was stabbed by someone on that goddamn stage. Also on the same damned stage we've got Palmer, the kid's girlfriend, and about forty extras. Our interviews with the extras gave us nothing so far, but deputies are still are finishing up those interviews. I keep going back to that girl, Eli. We've had her house under surveillance but nothing's turned up yet."

"Why don't you let me talk to her alone?"

"Why alone?"

"I think I can get more out of her because I'm a woman."

INTERVIEW REDUX WITH THE ROOMMATE

I eased the MG to the curb in front of Elisabeth Johnson's house in Tivoli. We needed a break in this jumbled mess of a case. I needed to hear something *useful*.

I knocked on the door. No one answered, so as before, I opened the screen and called out, "Eli? Eli! It's me, Lindsey! Eli!"

Footsteps down the stairs brought her face directly in front of mine, so near our noses nearly touched.

"To what do I owe the pleasure?" she asked and pulled me inside.

"I just wanted to talk to you again. I've been so worried about you since the sheriff and I first met you. I know you're going through a very rough time."

"Do you want a drink?" she asked.

I smiled. "Absolutely! Sounds great. What are you having?"

"Tequila."

We went into the kitchen and got the bottle and another shot glass. She put the salt shaker in her pocket along with the open lemon and a steak knife.

"We're all set," I said. "Where shall we sit?"

"Come on," she said, taking my hand. "I'll show you our secret terrace."

She led me upstairs into Brad's old room, opened one of the casement windows, and we stepped outside onto the roof of the back side of the house. Edging our way around a corner, we were between two dormers. There was a small bench, two children's chairs, and a few boards nailed together as a coffee table. At tree top level, we could see over the rooftops of Tivoli but no one could see us.

"What a sweet spot!" I said as we sat down. "Did you and Brad come up here to watch the stars?"

She nodded, sliced some lemon wedges and poured slugs of tequila. As she passed me the salt, I said, "It must be hard to love someone and hate them at the same time, isn't it?"

That was the right thing to say.

"Yes!" she exclaimed, her dark eyes flashing. "Yes! I never got a chance to make it right. We should have made up. I should have been cooler about the whole thing."

"That's why you feel so bad now. But it's not easy to be cool when a lover slips away. I've had that happen. It makes you want to---well, not kill them exactly, I'm not saying that, bad figure of speech. But it made me mad as hell. 'Who are you to dump me?' Right?"

"That's exactly right!" she answered. "At first I thought he was wonderful but then he started acting like a spoiled rich kid. Going to show *me* who's the *adult.*"

Eli gave each of us another shot.

"So how did you pay him back?"

She gave me a hard stare.

"I didn't say I did."

"Oh, come on! You must have done something. You're no pushover."

I poured us both another shot and cut lemon pieces. We salted the backs of our hands and threw back the shots. The fierceness of the lemon was matched by her voice. She threw her rind into the trees beyond us.

"No, you're right. I'm not a pushover. Two can play games. I called his father."

"His father?"

"Sure. I had met him a time or two and he'd given me enough of a look to let me know that he---well, let's just say he appreciated his son's taste in women. Then I seduced him."

"You seduced Brad's *father?*"

133

She shrugged. "Or vice versa. Whatever, it's done now."

"Have you seen him since Brad…since Brad died?

She looked smug. "He's coming over tonight."

It suddenly occurred to me that no one knew I was sitting on a roof with a young woman who was quite possibly a murderer.

"Coming over tonight? Well, I guess I better get going."

Eli grabbed my arm.

"No! Stay! I want him to see that I'm not just some college kid. Even *you* are taking an interest in me. I'm special. I'm not someone who gets used and then tossed aside."

"Perhaps some other time," I said and stood. Too late.

"Eli? Are you out here?" Louis Ruffin's head appeared around the corner.

"My, my," he smiled tightly. "I see we have a full house tonight."

"Doing your bit for grief counseling?" I asked tersely.

"Something like that. And you?"

"Cadging a drink. Consoling the lovelorn. We women understand about broken hearts."

"Broken hearts!" Ruffin laughed harshly. "That's the least of it, as I'm sure you realize. Please, sit down," he said. "I don't want you to go. I feel we have a lot to talk about. Don't you?"

He stepped toward me, roughly grasped my arm, and pushed me back down onto the bench.

"Hello up there! Room for one more?"

Bennett has a beautiful baritone. It had never sounded more wonderful. First his head popped up over the edge of the roof, then he hauled himself off a ladder that leaned against the house.

"Madame!" he cried. "We're late for dinner!" he said, taking my hand and pulling me around the dormer toward the open window. "Come along, dear! Mustn't keep the young ones from their studies."

134

Eli simply stared but Père Ruffin looked like a man whose plans to throw me off the roof had been interrupted.

◆◆◆◆◆

"How did you know where I was?" I asked, wobbling and shaky as Bennett steered me to the car.

"When you didn't come home, I called Paul. He said you'd gone to speak to the girl alone."

"How did you find the ladder?"

"There had to be some way to get out of that house other than the front door because the police had been watching it. The refrigerator blocks the back door out of the kitchen. But even when the look-out man saw no out-going traffic, sometimes Eli would arrive at the house when she was still supposed to be inside. A back-of-house window---or ladder---or a convenient tree---seemed the most obvious solution. I'm just glad it was a ladder! Paul called as I was en route and said that a man, now we know it was Ruffin, had just driven up."

"I hadn't figured the father as a cad, had you?"

"Frankly, I'm not surprised. Something told me he was a rotter when we met him at Huxley's. Too haughty. Too aloof."

"Yes, but would he kill his own son? Would *he and the girl* scheme to kill the boy?"

"Perhaps. If their affection for each other overwhelmed their affection for Brad."

When Bennett and I got home, I called Paul about my roof encounter with Eli, and Ruffin.

"Hmmm," Paul mused. "That puts the onus back on her. The kid's father was in the audience so he couldn't have stabbed the boy. But that weird girl could have."

"I find it astonishing that they were lovers. Very hard to believe. What a risk on Ruffin's part!"

Paul answered, "Well, dear, it's never good when the little head tells the big head what to do."

AN INTERVIEW WITH THE GRIEVING MOTHER

The next morning, before Paul's scheduled meeting with Ruffin for questioning, I called Dottie, asking if she would see me. She agreed at once.

I found her seated at a small desk in the library of the hotel.

As I sat down across from her, she said, "It seems a million years ago I was asking you to help me find and decorate a new house." She sighed and looked terribly sad. "What a disaster."

"I know this has been awful for you."

"Brad and I had always been so close. He seemed different lately, though. Like he had something weighing on his mind." We both sat silently for several moments.

"Where's Louis?" I asked.

"He's over meeting with Jason. Wanted to hold our hands some more, I guess."

Then she said, "Shall we have some tea?"

I nodded. "Would you like that?"

"Actually, I'd rather have a drink, I think. Would you join me if I had a little wine?"

"Absolutely, Dottie." Good old wine---the WD-40 of sticky interrogations.

As we drank, she began, "This is the end of the road for me, you know."

"Dottie, I'm so sorry..." I began but then only shook my head as no words came.

"Do you have children?" she asked.

"Afraid not," I answered.

"In many ways, I suppose they're just expensive clocks. I remember how young I was when Brad came. About the age he was now…or would have been in a year or so. Now I feel so old."

She paused and then began again.

"Marriage with Louis has been difficult. We married young after a very brief courtship. At the time I thought he was an incurable romantic, sweeping me off my feet, as they say, but in retrospect I see that I was essential to his plan. Every successful man---or in his case a man who was carefully *planning* on being very successful---needs a beautiful wife. And I was very beautiful. And very rich. The perfect combination, right?"

"How were you rich?" I asked.

"My people have lived in Mississippi and the Delta for generations. In the decades when cotton was King, the family grew a hell of a lot of cotton. In the 1840's, they invested in the Hopson Planting Company who mechanized the entire process---planting, cultivating, harvesting, and baling. They also partnered with an English company who manufactured cloth. That made them enough money to ride out the Civil War in Paris after the Union blockade of 1861 stopped shipping altogether."

"I'm from the South, too." I said. "Your family didn't support the absurd valor of the Southern cause? Didn't take a stand against the War of Northern Aggression?" I shook my head sadly. "I find the Civil War so tragic, I can't bear to think about it."

She nodded. "My family thought it was a lost cause, as anyone who honestly faced the realities of the time would have.

"After the war, my people returned and, like every other plantation family, supported the sharecropping movement, with one big difference: Share the wealth, not just the crops. By 1870, the South was producing more cotton than it had in 1860, we were back to supplying England and we cut the former slaves in on the cloth profits. And then the timber business took off. Lots of pine trees in Mississippi and our former slaves took to running kilns and sawmills with considerable success."

She smiled. "I'm rather proud to say my great-great grandparents not only prospered but picked up some new ideas about social equality in France.

"Years later, by the time the bottom fell out of the cotton market in the late 1940's and early 50's, my parents had sold or leased out their land and put that money into Coca-Cola stock and Ford dealerships. My dad was an Eagle Scout and at a Jamboree he met a kid named Walton. Sam and he stayed in touch and Dad was an early investor in his company. Times were good. That's the money that financed Louis's foray into wildcat prospecting."

"His rare earth phase?" I asked. "He said that was a summer job."

"A summer job that lasted for seven or eight years."

"Did he know Franklin?"

"I believe their paths did cross at one point, years ago. It's such a narrow field, I suppose everybody knows everybody else."

"Nothing more than that?"

She shrugged. "I don't really know. For years, Louis was so gung-ho about the mining, the metals, the deals. He made some money but nothing substantial came of it. Then he suddenly dropped the whole thing and applied for graduate school in architecture. I didn't question it, one generally does not question Louis, but it was agreeable to me because it meant he would be at home instead of travelling constantly."

"Lot of money in rare earth."

"Now there is. But thirty years ago he was ahead of the curve. And Louis was just one man. He was not aligned with any big mining firms, and because the majority of my money was tied up in trusts, we didn't really have the millions in cash it takes to buy the futures, or mine the products, or ride out the waiting time between extraction and sales."

"How old were you when Brad was born?"

"Almost thirty. We'd tried for years but I was never able to become pregnant. Louis, of course, refused to have any kind of test, and refused to take the *in vitro* route. I started the adoption process on my own, forging his signature on documents."

New news.

"But surely interviews with *both* prospective parents would have been a part of the adoption process?" I asked.

She nodded. "Definitely. That's when Louis hit the roof. But I explained that I wanted a child and if he wanted to continue to rely on me for support until he got his practice established, then he'd need to go along with the adoption."

"Dottie, where did the adoption take place? What agency did you use?"

"Why is that important?"

"I'm not sure that it is. But it might be. Will you tell me?"

"It was an agency in New York City. Chadwick-Smythe. They've been around for a hundred years, started out rescuing foundlings, babies left in baskets on church steps."

"I see. Did Brad know he was adopted? Did anyone else know he was adopted?"

She shook her head. "I never told Brad. I'm sure he wondered why Louis was often aloof. Oh, he had his occasional paternal streaks, probably to please me, but generally he was a rather distant father. But I never commented on that either. Did Brad guess? Perhaps. We'll never know now. At any rate, this is the end of the road for me, in this life anyway. I'm leaving Louis."

She finished her wine and refilled both our glasses.

"Why do you say it's the 'end of the road'? Surely it's just a new chapter. You're still a young woman."

Dottie smiled. "You're right. That's a better way of looking at it. Brad's death has finally made me face how empty my life has become---and made me admit that hoping for any relationship with Louis is not only futile, but ridiculous.

139

"I still have a law practice, not that I'm very interested in it anymore. There are philanthropies I'd like to pursue, places I'd like to visit, friendships I want to renew---and I also need to do a better job of looking after myself, not just my psychological well-being, but my health in general."

I frowned.

"What? I mean, you look fabulous! The picture of good health! Hard to believe you might be...unwell..." I squeezed her hand. "Do you want to talk about it?"

"Nothing so terrible. I just have a mild form of epilepsy. Actually," she exclaimed, "I am sort of a medical mystery!"

"How so?" I asked.

Dottie began to explain. "Some children have what's called 'absence seizures.' They're *petit mal* rather than *grand mal*. My illness, however, is also a form of what's called 'photosensitive epilepsy,' the sort that usually triggers full-on seizures. My medication manages it to the extent that I just sort of black out for a few moments. I've done this since I was a child. Most kids grow out of it. Anyone watching me during an episode would assume, as I sit staring blankly into space, that my mind had simply wandered off somewhere. I don't fall over, I don't writhe on the floor. I just sit and stare."

"How long do these last?" I asked.

"Not too long, half a minute or less usually, unless I continue to be exposed to whatever triggered it in the first place."

"Like what? What triggers these episodes?"

"Unfortunately, any number of things. That's the 'photosensitive' aspect. Usually something to do with *light*. I was never the most popular girl during the disco revival because the strobe lights turned me into a zombie! Laser light shows at rock concerts or, say, during the Super Bowl halftime, I'm not a big fan of those. Anything with rapid flashes of light."

"So if you continue to be exposed...what happens then?"

"Then I can have several episodes in a row, lasting for some time. The first time the multiple episodes occurred, Louis and Brad and I were at the Fête de Genève, the big fireworks show around the lake. That lasted about an hour and I missed the whole damn thing!"

PROCEDURAL IMPROV

After our tête à tête, Dottie headed over to Brad's house to collect his belongings. I had about an hour before our appointment with Louis Ruffin.

Something in my left elbow suggested a closer look at the Ruffins' room would be in order. Paul was minutes away in the incident room. I texted him to meet me at the hotel.

As Paul was climbing out of his car, Joe came over to greet us.

"How's it going?" he asked.

"Like to ask you about cooking," I said. "Recipes are great, but do you ever improvise?"

"You mean make it up as I go along? Sure. All good chefs do that."

"Good cops do, too," I said.

"Meaning…?"

"Meaning Paul and I would like to have an unofficial look around the Ruffins' room. The father is at the college meeting with the president and I just left the mother. She's gone over to Brad's house to pick up his things."

Joe walked us upstairs. Unlocking the door, he said, "My mother runs our housekeeping. I'm going to station her by the window down there at the end of the hall. She'll be able to see everybody coming or going. If either Ruffin shows up, she'll get you out of there and down the service stairs. Good cooking."

He held the door open and we went in.

Paul said, "Very good idea, Lindsey. I have trained you well," as he and I entered and surveyed the room. Two double beds. Several suitcases. An armoire. A Sheridan chest. Two closets.

"What exactly are we expecting to find?" Paul asked.

"I don't know. Something told me we should look around. So look around."

"Fine," Paul said. "I'll start going through the drawers."

"The day I met him, Ruffin mentioned wanting to buy a house up here because he likes fly fishing. Here's his tackle."

"That should be very revealing, dear."

There were waders; nothing inside either leg. The well-used creel was expensive and English, split willow with a leather harness and clasp. About forty colorful, feathered flies were in a leaved canvas zippered pouch. A separate canvas pouch held a packet of waterproof matches, a fish scaler, a roll of gauze and some tape, and some adhesive rubber patches. I guess those were in case his waders sprang a leak. The matches in case he needed to make a fire. The gauze in case of a minor accident. And the scaler blade for field-cleaning his trout. A serious angler and a thoughtful packer.

Paul called out, "This is her stuff in the bureau. You go through that. I'll take the armoire." Our chivalrous sheriff.

As one might expect, Dottie travelled with beautiful lingerie. Silk blouses. Handsome dresses and suits. Nothing stood out, nothing looked like a clue.

"I'm blanking over her stuff," I said. "What have you got?"

"The guy is a clothes horse. Nice jackets and trousers. Very nice. Some labels say they were made for him. Drawers show him to be a briefs man. That almost proves he is a criminal," Paul sniggered. I gather he is a boxer man.

"Also he's got a pair of golf gloves but no clubs or golf shoes. Just some fancy black suede driving mocs. Low quarter brogans. Brown dress shoes. Blue suit, light tan suit, tux, sport coat, a few knit shirts. Dress shirts still in packaging from the cleaners. Is there a laundry bag?"

I looked in the closet. A nylon drawstring bag lying on the floor of the closet held some crumpled shirts, a pair of chinos, a travelling shoe-shine kit, and a yard or so of muslin for polishing.

Paul turned to me and said, "I don't believe we have found a smoking gun. Do you see anything to follow up on?"

"Not as much as I had hoped. Let's go grill the guy. Maybe that will turn up something useful."

A CONVERSATION WITH PÈRE RUFFIN

On our way in to question Ruffin, I filled Paul in on what I had learned from Dottie.

"Ruffin told us he had a *summer job* in minerals. Well, he didn't. He was a minerals wildcatter for about seven years. He must have met Franklin. Not that many people were working in that field back then."

"What does that have to do with anything?" Paul snapped.

"Just for a second think about this---maybe back then Ruffin was onto a big find, or was close to making a deal, but couldn't pull it off. Maybe Franklin took it away from him. Maybe Ruffin killed Cassandra to create horrible publicity for Franklin. His sorts of deals need trust. Bad publicity, Franklin's companies could take a hit."

Paul stared at me. "You think this is a business vendetta? Give me a break."

"Why not? We're not exactly awash in motives."

We walked into the interrogation room where Ruffin sat twirling a pen in his hands.

"Tell us about your wildcatting days," Paul said.

"Fishing expedition, Sheriff?" sneered Ruffin.

"It's hot stuff now, batteries for cars, for solar, wind, tidal storage. But back when you were prospecting, what, thirty years ago, not much going on. And not many players. Did you ever run across Franklin O'Connell?" I asked.

"Long time ago. Our paths may have crossed a time or two."

I asked, "What was your biggest deal?"

"Out in the Mojave desert. Found a nice claim. Needed money to bring it out. Would have been the payoff for everything, years of research. I'd had several minor lucky strikes but it all seemed to come together with this one. But I needed a partner with money to make it happen."

"So you called....Franklin?"

"First I called some other people, but they were sharks. Wanted the whole damn thing, giving me pennies on the tonnage. So I called O'Connell."

"How'd that work out?" Paul asked.

"I got him to meet me at the site, in California, the Clark Mountain Range."

"Where is that?" I asked.

"Right on the border with Nevada."

"When was this?" Paul asked.

"Late Eighties. I brought O'Connell in to look at it. He asked if I knew what was going on in China. They were getting into the business big time. We talked the whole deal through. He decided not to go for it. Said we were not going to generate the returns within the time frame he needed. Told me all markets have cycles and that I just happened to be at the tail end of this one. He said it would come back, as the demand grew---which we both knew it would. We could have made millions. But he moved on, left me hanging out there."

"Sounds like a business decision to me," Paul said. "No reflection on you, just a comment on the ways the markets were running. Tough to fight China."

Ruffin slammed his fist on the table. "I had contacts, defense people, energy people. I could have made it work. We could have made millions! Millions! But he wanted a sure thing. So he went with wind, waves, and light bulbs. How goddamn exciting is that? Frigging light bulbs."

"So you sort of hate the guy, if I'm hearing you correctly?" Paul asked with faux innocence. "You wanted rare

146

earth metals, whatever the hell those are, you wanted to move on the project and O'Connell didn't. Bad break for you but that's business. Nothing personal, as the Corleones say, right?"

I asked, "Did anything ever happen with the deposits you found?"

Ruffin leaned back in his chair and smiled. "They stayed in the ground for thirty-something years. Then about a year ago, O'Connell bought the whole place. How's that for the last laugh? Bastard."

"When did you last speak to Franklin O'Connell?"

"We said hello at the dinner before the theatre."

"How long have you known Eli Johnson?"

"I met her a couple of weeks ago."

"Do you want to take a Mulligan on that one, Louis?"

"A what?"

"A do-over. When did you meet Eli Johnson?"

"Christ, we've met several of Brad's friends, hard to be precise."

"When did you start sleeping with your son's girlfriend?" Paul asked.

Ruffin's eyes flashed and he snapped, "Who the hell said I was 'sleeping with her'? We've had a couple of rolls in the hay, nothing more. The last time I looked, there was nothing illegal about that."

"Maybe Brad's girlfriend had a more permanent arrangement in mind," I suggested.

"Meaning what?" Ruffin answered.

"Meaning that killing Brad was a way for you and Eli to be together without having unattractive father/son scenes," I offered.

He snorted. "Oh, please! She's a kid. Surely she knows this was just sex. How could I be interested in a twinkie? And I doubt she's got the guts to stab anyone. Although, 'hell hath no fury...'" He trailed off.

"It seemed serious enough for you---or the two of you---to want to throw me off the roof," I snapped.

"Don't be melodramatic, little miss deputy sheriff."

"Is your wife aware this is going on?" Paul asked.

"I haven't the vaguest but if she does, I'm sure her reaction would be, so what? She's lost interest so there's not a lot of sex left in our marriage. Hasn't been for years. That is not exactly unusual. But there is more to a marriage than sex. I have a beautiful wife, I love her, and I am devoted to her. I have no intention of leaving her. And could I ask for my son's body? I may not be much of a husband or father in your eyes but I do know my wife needs to plan a funeral."

◆◆◆◆◆

Paul sent Ruffin away and followed me home for a much-needed drink.

Bennett obliged us with rum punch on the porch. In contrast to our glum mood, the river sparkled in the early evening light and a breeze played through the yard.

Paul sighed. I sighed.

"What a muddle," I muttered. Paul rubbed his eyes.

"The two of you look exceedingly the worse for wear," Bennett said. "Perhaps it would clear your heads to recount what is known and unknown thus far. Who could our killers be?"

Paul said, "This is a complicated mess. Lindsey, what are your ideas?"

I said nothing, continued sipping and staring at Catskill Creek. Four kayaks glided past. A sailboat moved steadily downriver, running with the tide and the breeze.

"Let's take the boy first," Bennett insisted. "That would seem straightforward. He was killed onstage. Must have been a cast member. Or his girlfriend. Or Palmer, the director. All the suspects were onstage."

"Then there is unfortunate Cassandra Chappelle. She was given poison, almost certainly at the O'Connells'. A chef was also murdered, we assume to facilitate the poisoning. We assume the interloper took his place and planted the aconite. Who might that have been? Francesca was there. The Ruffins were there. The mystery chef was there. That's four."

"But why suspect the Ruffins?" I asked. "What possible reason would they have for poisoning Cassandra? Palmer was at the O'Connells' very briefly, leaving immediately after a drink to go to the theatre to ensure all was in order. But again, why kill Brad? He seemed genuinely fond of the boy. He wept when we first met him after Brad's death."

I gestured to Bennett for a refill and then turned to Paul. "This may be nothing but it seems odd."

"What?"

"How could Ruffin have a pair of golf gloves and not know what a Mulligan is?"

BAXTER'S WILL

The convenient thing about Skype is seeing people face to face. The inconvenient thing about Skype is the lag and the feeling that you're conversing with someone underwater on another planet.

Paul and I settled ourselves in his Bard office and called the Ojai law firm to discuss the covenants in the will of Cassandra's late husband, Baxter.

"What were the terms of Baxter's will?" Paul asked

"Everything was left to Cassandra," said Managing Partner A.

"Outright?" I asked.

"That gets complicated," replied Managing Partner B.

"Essentially," he continued, "she had an allowance each year, a ceiling beyond which she could not spend without the executor's approval. Before he died, Baxter worked out an annual budget---housing, food, clothes, the necessities, and also giving her money for her interests---travel, scholarly endowments, etc."

"And upon her death?" I asked.

"Whatever remained was to be divided equally between his two children---after giving Cassandra some latitude about bequests of her own. The problem was, the estate was no longer getting the returns on the principal it had enjoyed for many years---and which Baxter had anticipated. He was well-diversified, but 2008 took a bite out of the principal and so did the market's later fluctuations. The value would come back, of course, but terms of the will included no index tying Cassandra's spending to the diminishment of the corpus."

"The what?" Paul asked.

Partner A adjusted his tortoise frames. "Even though the overall size of the estate had dropped, she was under no constraints about continuing to spend at the same level."

"And was she spending heavily?"

"Yes, she was. She advised us she planned on buying the house she had rented up in your area. The price was terribly out of line but since she had already told the owner to stop showing it, she had to have it, you can imagine how that affected our negotiating position."

"How many stepkids are there and where do they live?" Paul asked.

Partner B answered, "There's a son and a daughter. The daughter is in New York, the son is in Connecticut."

"Do they need money?" Paul asked.

"The daughter is an occasional actress. She is married to a playwright who is famous but only stages a production every ten or so years. Baxter set up trusts for the grandkids' schools well before his death, but still, life gets more expensive every day.

"The son is some sort of consultant, I think. He is low profile for us. His sister is the one who has called us repeatedly about the terms of the will---and who, I might add, has been in touch several times since the widow Chappelle's death."

Paul hedged, "You can't do anything until we get the results of the autopsy."

"Autopsy!!" both Partners A and B gasped. "Do we understand you are treating this as a suspicious death?"

"Your first clue on that was when you got a call from a sheriff, I would think," Paul barked. "We'll be in touch."

We shut Skype off and Paul said, "I can see one big motive in her late husband's will---his kids inherit. She gets to make some bequests and that would be a nice windfall for somebody but the bulk goes to the daughter in the city and the brother. Still, I gotta believe *her* will is the one we need. Lindsey, go find it."

I nodded.

"But still," I began, "even though both children were worried about Cassandra's running through the majority of Baxter's money, I can't see how either could have poisoned her," I said. "Neither was at the O'Connells' dinner that night. Were they?"

Paul said, "I think we better verify that."

I nodded, "There is that theatre connection."

"Tomorrow morning, we head down to New York, dear."

A peck on the cheek and Paul was gone.

I went back over to Cassandra's on automatic pilot. I felt like a person walking through a room in the dark. All the clues had to be right in front of us but we couldn't put them in the right order. A sort of detective dyslexia had settled over us.

Magda let me in.

"I've just made myself some coffee," she said. "Vood you like a cup?"

"I'd love that, Magda, thanks." I followed her into the kitchen where she poured. I suggested we sit for minute.

"Magda, I'm curious to know how Cassandra spent her time. What did she do with her days?"

"Every morning she did her yoga. Then she ate her breakfast, alvays the same think. Cereal, black coffee, and yogurt vith a bowl of fruit."

"Did she go grocery shopping herself?"

"Most of the time she did. She loved to go to the farm stands and the pick-your-own places. She vanted all heirloom tomatoes, the uglier the better. 'Purple tomatoes!' she kept saying. And she drove all over the county going to the goat farms and sheep farms. Loved that. She'd get cheeses, foie gras, berries of all kinds. She'd tell me, 'Magda! I'm a foodie!' "

"What about the flower gardens? Did she take an interest in them?"

"Not so much. She hired people to tell her what to plant where and then they did it."

"What else did she do?"

"She'd go to the Kaatsbahn barns for the dancing, although she didn't think it amounted to much, said a lot of it vas not modern dance, was just bad dance, not that I vood know one way or the other. She vent to the Upstate to see hart films. Ant of course, she vent into New York to see plays, concerts, lectures."

"Did she go to things at Bard very often?" I asked.

"Vell, from some months back she vent to the school, vas speaking to der classes about how to be an actress. I think that's how she met some of those twerps who started coming around."

"Thanks, Magda. I think I'll look through the office some more and see if I can find that will today."

I returned to Cassandra's office and began to rummage around.

Looking through her calendar, I saw lunches, dinners, doctors, trips into town.

Her files were endless piles of theatrical and performance ephemera. Programs from every sort of venue. The ABT was a favorite, also Carnegie Hall, and anything at Lincoln Center. Stuck in the back was a program from The Players Club for an evening honoring Edward Albee. A signed Bobby Short photograph. Hundreds of ticket stubs. A picture of Cassandra with Dolly Parton and Mick Jagger at the Bottom Line. A menu from Les Pleiades. A VIP pass from Hippopotamus. A dried gardenia corsage. A postcard from Hal Prince, notes from Sondheim and Lloyd Webber.

Nothing noteworthy jumped out at me. It all just seemed an indiscriminate bunch of memorabilia kept by an actress who couldn't bear to part with any memento of her life.

Moving over to a third file cabinet, I found Cassandra had also kept a vast archive of her career, from childhood, no less, onward. Hundreds of file folders held sheaves of newspaper clippings about her recitals as a five year old, her singing the lead in a school play at ten, her teenage performance at a Los Angeles television station's talent show. On and on. Ye gods! Did I really have to wade through all this rubbish?

And there were programs from the few minor legitimate theatrical productions she'd appeared in, as well as a slew of regional shows and traveling companies. All of this slavery, and, according to Huxley, that's what it amounted to, culminated in *Harlot*.

I found a massive album devoted to the *Harlot* era. Publicity photographs of the cast, interviews in the *Times* and other New York dailies, features from *Life*, *Look*, *Time*, *Photoplay*, *Variety*, *New York Magazine*, *Interview*.

I finally came across the Playbill from *Harlot* and began reading the thing from back to front. What a relic of a vanished New York! The ads for restaurants and watering holes long gone, ridiculously dated clothing advertisements from long-closed department stores, now-vintage cars, fragrances that were no longer sold.

I got to the cast c.v.'s listing the parts they had played on Broadway and Off.

In tiny type below the synopsis of the acts---'There will be one 15 minute intermission'---a small paragraph listed the understudies.

The understudy for the lead dancer was Donald Palmer.

ANOTHER VISIT WITH DONALD PALMER

I tore over to the College to confront Palmer.

Seeing me banging on his door, Millie, the drama Department secretary called out from her desk on the landing, "He's not in. If you need him, go look in the Spiegeltent. He has a class there in about half an hour."

The Spiegeltent, a part of Bard's Summer Music Festival for several years, is a portable Belgian behemoth built in 1920 of 3,000 pieces of wood, mirrors, canvas and stained glass. To my mind the flamboyant structure has always looked like a vaudeville producer ate magic mushrooms in Bavaria, went to a carpentry class taught by Breughel figures, and created his dream venue for Oktoberfest on Staten Island. But I am in the minority; audiences love the mittel-something-or-other ambience.

In its almost hundred-year lifetime, this very structure has hosted some of the world's greatest performing artists, including Marlene Dietrich, who famously sang 'Falling in Love Again' in it during the 1930s.

The Spiegeltent tours the world, transported from festival to festival in shipping containers, then assembled on site at each location. Here at Bard, its stage, dance floor, booths and banquettes with velvet and brocade detailing have proven wildly popular, a little touch of the Ardennes *cum* Kit Kat Klub in ye olde Hudson Valley. Cabaret acts, singers, comedians, and acrobats from around the world come to perform their avant garde and risqué routines, to say nothing of a separate children's program. They haven't booked snake handlers yet, but wait a few seasons.

In the daytime, the Bard drama faculty uses the Spiegeltent for summer school classes and drama workshops. I walked across the Commons and saw workmen wrestling planters of shrubbery into position on the Spiegeltent's terrace.

Palmer was backstage in a tiny dressing room applying a false nose with spirit glue above a bristly false beard. He wore a wig hat with his purple fright wig combed and ready on a stand beside him.

"The triumphant return of the Brothers Grimm, I presume?" I remarked, squeezing in beside him.

Keeping his eyes on the mirror, he said, "Listen, I'd like to talk but I have a class in fifteen minutes."

"I'm just here to chew a quick bit of fat," I said. "Tell me what it's like to teach here. How's the money?"

"You can get my salary from Jason."

"Don't you even get a summer break? Or are the kids always underfoot?"

"We who teach, enjoy teaching. We don't think of them as 'underfoot.' "

"Any travel plans this year?"

"Don't beat around the bush. If you want to know something, just ask me," Palmer said crossly.

"Did you ever work with Cassandra?"

"God, no. She was gone by the time I got my first part."

"No, she wasn't. You understudied in *Harlot*. Why lie?" I waited.

For a moment he continued roughing in an eyebrow, then slammed down the grease pencil.

"What difference does that make? It was years ago. Decades ago! She was the star, I was an understudy who went on once, if memory serves. The stars and the understudies were not fast friends. If she were alive and you asked her, 'who is Donald Palmer?' she'd give you the blankest of stares."

157

"Palmer, cut the crap. You invited Cassandra to teach a master class up here. She also sat in on your classes to critique student monologues. 'Would you please give the kids a few pointers, Madame Harlot?' That's where she met Brad. Did you have them do a scene together? Is that how it started?"

"How what started? Look, you are barking up the wrong tree. This is absurd."

"Am I? It's a simple matter to verify that? What about the times you saw Cassandra at the Madalin?"

"Fine! All right! We saw each other a few times for dinner at the Madalin. It was not my idea! Several weeks ago, Jason called me, said he had a potential underwriter for *Henry V* who wanted to meet the director to assure herself of the 'theatrical integrity' of the piece, whatever the hell that is. However, when a possible underwriter is at hand, it seemed a perfectly reasonable request. I arrived at the Madalin for lunch at 1:30. Cassandra arrived with Jason. When I saw it was she, I stood up, preparing to leave. They both interpreted my standing as merely manners. She excused herself to powder her nose. I turned to leave and Jason ordered me to sit the hell down. The luncheon was uneventful. Out of the blue, Jason suggested I invite her to give an informal 'Master Class.' I was flabbergasted but *she* was flattered. I don't know how much the kids got out of her advice, but it was ninety minutes, not the revival of an old friendship. Got it?"

"No, that's not quite true."

"Says who?" Palmer snapped.

"Says Joe, the owner of the Madalin. He called you and Cassandra regulars. Said you had 'date nights'."

"Sometimes assuring a backer of the integrity of the piece takes a little time. And may I correct your erroneous impression, those few evenings were not 'date nights,' they were two old pros talking theatre. It happens. Mostly we talked about *Henry V*, the speeches, the blocking, the technical effects."

Undeterred, I continued, "Brad's roommate says he had a patron. I'm wondering if it was you?"

"His patron?! You must be mad! How the hell could it be me!? I don't have that kind of money!"

"Just as well," I said. "Even if he hadn't been murdered, the poor boy didn't have long to live anyway."

"What on earth are you talking about?!" Palmer shook his head in exasperation.

"Oh, you didn't know? He had Creutzfeldt-Jacob. Might have lasted another few years but maybe not."

"What the hell is that?" he scowled.

"It's an hereditary disease. It's on his dad's side of the family. It's like early Alzheimer's, only faster."

Palmer leaned toward me until his face was a few inches from mine. "Let me get this straight. You're telling me Brad inherited some fatal disease from *Louis's family?*"

"Right. Sad, eh?"

"That is total bullshit! I don't know where you got that idea but he has no blood relationship to his father's *or* mother's parents. Brad was adopted."

"How do you know that?"

"Dottie came up last winter, alone, to see him in *Midsummer.* After the show, the cast and several of us went out for drinks. She and I wound up together at the end of a very long evening, and after a great deal of wine, as people are wont to do, we were sharing our life stories. She told me then. Told me the boy did not know, so I never mentioned it to him. But tell me where you heard this line of crap?"

"Can't remember now. I'll have to check my notes."

FLASHBACKS WITH JASON PRIESTLY

Leaving Palmer, it was late afternoon when I barged into Jason's office.

Surprised at my abrupt arrival, Jason asked, "What have you got?"

"I'd like to know more about Donald Palmer? I think the two of you went to high school together? 'Prepped' was the way he put it."

"Right. In Lakeville. We were in the same dorm as freshmen and the same suite after that."

"Did you keep in touch after school?"

"Off and on. He went to New Haven, I went to Cambridge. We saw each other at football games."

"He went to Yale for drama?"

Jason nodded.

"What about when he was working in New York? Did you go down for any plays?"

"Of course I did. Love the theatre!"

"When did you meet your wife?"

"I met her at Oxford. What does that have to do with anything?"

"How close were you and Don?"

Jason pushed away from his desk, shoved his hands into his pockets.

"I'll give you what you're angling for. I might as well, since you'll never get it out of Palmer. He and I have been close friends for many years. He's a great brain and a marvelous actor. He was working as an understudy in *Harlot*. I'd come down to New York fairly often for visits and to see the shows. He and

Cassandra had just begun seeing each other, but seemed to have something good going for them. I'd go so far as to say Don was falling in love with her. Mind you, this was while she was also involved with Coen. That man damned near ruined her life."

"How'd she get away from him, by the way?" I asked.

"He came to her dressing room one night, slapped her, and Cassandra's dresser, Magda, threw a jar of turpentine in his face. Just missed his eyes. Feisty little thing, that dresser. After that, things cooled off with the old letch."

"Tell me more about Cassandra and Palmer and you."

"The three of us used to go out after their show, grab dinner and a drink, maybe go clubbing. One night we had gotten some grass from somewhere, and went back to Don's place. Cassandra lured us both into bed, said she'd had a boyfriend--- that would be Coen---who fancied threesomes and wouldn't we like to try it? Hell, we both had skins full of wine, were high as kites, and an orgy seemed like a fabulous idea! What the hell did we know about it? But, mercurial as ever, once Palmer and I had stripped off and hopped under the sheets, Cassandra turned on us and called us pansies. It finished her relationship with Don. Too bad. Not only did he care for her but she could have been a big help to his career."

"Why the hell open old wounds by having her sit in on some of his classes?"

Jason laughed derisively. "I doubt she even remembered it. That fleeting debacle was just one more casually destructive turn in her life's work of spoiling it for anyone within her reach."

"Maybe you worried she'd be telling tales about you up here. That could have been embarrassing to The Great Man you've now become."

"Hardly! It was Cassandra who needed to Be Somebody up here. The Great Patron. She was unlikely to queer the deal, if you will. And I was certainly not afraid of any tales she might tell from, what, thirty years ago when Don and I were twentysomethings and the Age of Aquarius was still dawning. This is a liberal Northeastern college, remember, not Bob Jones or Oral Roberts."

"You were at the dinner. You had the opportunity to poison her."

It sounded incredibly lame even to me and Jason roared with laughter.

"Murdering my underwriters?! Forgive me! Let's have a drink on that, shall we, Lindsey?"

He moved to the sideboard and poured two glasses of scotch.

I drank, toasting to myself silently, 'Here's to another dead end.'

After I left Jason, I sat in my car and called Palmer.

"Just another few questions. Were you at the theatre before the show?"

With extreme irritation, he replied, "Of course I was! You don't think a bloody thing like that happens without someone calming nerves, giving last minute direction, and making sure all the students know their marks and cues?"

"Jason has told us about what happened when the three of you were kids in New York, the time you wound up in bed together."

His voice dripping with sarcasm, Palmer replied, "How kind of him to volunteer that little chestnut. Back then, I suppose you could say I was a dabbler. Bisexual, I told myself. She was so beautiful. Jason was so beautiful. I rather lost my heart. I thought I could have it both ways, have it all.

"If I had wanted to kill her, believe me, I could have. I chose to forgive her and forget her.

"To the point, you seem to have mislaid the fact that I have not seen or spoken to the woman in thirty years. Our rapprochement, if you are daft enough to think that's what it

162

was, was because Jason wanted to lock her in as a benefactor to the college. That's it. Have you got that?"

And he slammed down the phone.

CASSANDRA'S NEXT-OF-KIN

Paul and I took the 6.30 morning drool train out of Hudson into New York to meet Cassandra's late husband Baxter's actress daughter, Erica Trenton, and her husband, the playwright David Baer.

As Paul and I disembarked in Penn Station, the subterranean travesty built following the sacrilegious destruction of the original Penn Station---McKim, Mead and White's homage to the Baths of Caracalla---it occurred to me to ask you, gentle reader, to write to your government representatives with the simple message: We can do better.

The actress and author lived downtown on Tenth Street between Fifth and Sixth, possibly my favorite block in the Village.

The south side of mid-Tenth Street has James Renwick's 1895 'English Terrace Row,' the first group of houses in the city to forego the high Dutch stoop. 'Terrace' is the English term for a row of identical houses, such as we see in the Kensington and Paddington areas of London. New Yorkers who visited England's capital in the mid 19th century so admired the style they adopted it upon their return to New York.

Among the customary brownstones, several substantial mansions line the street, their grand scale unusual for the Village. Most are Italianate but number 12 is an exception, with its rounded bay window, and its early division into apartments rather than remaining a single family residence. One of the early habitants, Emily Post, the very witty Etiquette Czarina, entertained President Wilson at Thanksgiving in 1915 and witnessed his proposal of marriage to his second wife.

Just across the street, the Trenton/Baer house was a handsome brick four-storey with a leaded glass, canted bay window framed by an ancient wisteria vine.

Erica Trenton met us at the door. She had been in several successful movies and stage productions but they'd been stretched out over a few decades so she was not a 'star' by today's media-driven standards. She was slender, wore a beige hopsack tunic and several knobby necklaces over black leggings. She had a pleasant if not exactly beautiful face framed by gray-blonde curls. She seemed amused that we were calling on her in connection with Cassandra's death.

As we walked upstairs, she asked, "So what exactly is this about? You came all the way down here to have me tell you how sorry I am The Great Star Cass popped?"

Paul began, "This is a routine inquiry in connection with your stepmother's death."

"Don't call that greedy bitch my 'stepmother,' " she snarled. She gestured to Paul and me to sit down in a book-lined, magazine and newspaper strewn parlor. Lighting a cigarette, she laughed and said, "There was not a motherly bone in that witch's body. Oh! Wait! Let me take that back! She *was* motherly---but to my father who was old enough to be her grandfather when they married. The old fool. Do you want a drink?"

After that outburst, Paul nodded at me to keep the ball rolling, so I said, "No, thank you. I'm sorry, the sheriff and I did not realize you and Cassandra were not close. She and I had become friendly, she'd asked for my help in redoing her house in Rhinebeck. She always spoke very fondly of you," I lied merrily.

"Like hell! She couldn't stand me. We'd never have seen a penny of Dad's if he hadn't set aside money for my kids' schools."

The front door opened and a man's voice in the stairwell called, "Erica, who are you talking to?"

"Nobody!" she shouted. "Just two cops who are quizzing me about why we don't have photos of Cassandra all over the mantle."

Barreling around the corner into the study, a fellow with wispy sandy hair wearing a chino suit and white button-down with a madras tie stuck out his hand and said, "I'm David Baer. What can we do for you? Sit back down. You want coffee? Pinot Grigio? Malbec?"

Paul said, "No, thanks." We both sat back down.

"When did you last see Cassandra?" Paul asked.

Peeling off his jacket, Baer walked over to the bar, and poured himself and Erica glasses of bourbon and added splashes of water. "Hell's bells, I thought that's why you're here. We were at the play the night she died."

Do tell, I thought, and said, "Why go? I mean, your wife said you couldn't stand her."

Baer laughed. "Are you familiar with that old saw, hope springing eternal? I've got a script for a new show. Looking for backers. She not only has money, she *knows* a lot of people with money who fancy themselves angels. Investments in the theatre don't always work out, of course, but fat cats can always use a few more deductions, and, of course, a few seats on the aisle. I sent her the script, and she said she 'saw some merit in it,' like she's Charles frigging Isherwood."

He threw himself into a chair and lit a cigarette.

"I'm ashamed to say I even wrote a part for her, a sort of Madame Arcati turn. Of course, what was good enough for Angela Lansbury was *nowhere* good enough for Cassandra, heavens no! I'm sure she was waiting for me to suggest she was *perfect* for the ingénue's role, with perhaps a bit of tinkering, just a decade or four. God, what an egotist."

"When did you last see Cassandra?" Paul repeated.

"Hadn't *seen* her in months, years even. Can you recall, darling?"

Erica shook her head. "Have no idea. But I think I maybe caught a glimpse of her at Madame Tussaud's?" She giggled merrily and drank deeply.

Baer continued, "Ours was an arm's length relationship. Nothing closer than long distance phone calls, the longer the better."

"So the evening at *Henry V* was your first meeting in quite a while?"

"Who said anything about meeting?" Erica snorted.

"She sent us tickets and we went but we didn't see her, not to speak to her. We were to meet her for lunch the next day. I gather there was a big dinner before the show to which we were pointedly not invited. We saw her enter the theatre, acting like Beyoncé *cum* Lady Gaga, flouncing and waving. Then at the intermission, along with everyone else, saw her keel over."

"Tsk tsk," said Erica Trenton.

"An opportunity lost," added Baer.

Paul continued, "What time did you get up to Rhinebeck?"

"We drove up the night before," Baer answered. "Stayed in town. Beekman Arms."

"Did you have dinner before the theatre?"

"Yeah, we ate across the street at Le Petit Bistro."

"Can anyone vouch for that?" Paul asked.

Baer smiled. "Probably. Ask them if they remember the guy who drank the '82 Pomerol."

"Have you been to the theatre at Bard before?" I asked.

Baer nodded. "They do some interesting things at their summer festivals. Very creative little hotbed. I have been considering doing a table reading of my new play up there, just kicking the idea around with the drama department."

"That would be Donald Palmer?" I asked.

He nodded. "Yes, that's right. You know Palmer?"

Paul answered, "We've gotten to know him as we look into another death, of one of the actors that night."

167

Baer shook his head, frowning. "A lot of mayhem for one evening."

"Do you know if your brother and Cassandra had been in touch?" I asked.

"Little Baxter Junior?" Erica lit another cigarette. "I doubt it. She was the same witch's tit to him as she was to us."

"He's up in Connecticut, right?" I asked.

She nodded.

"What does he do for a living? Some sort of consultant?" Paul asked.

"Oh, no, he's in the theatre, as well!" At this, they both howled.

"What's funny?" Paul asked.

"Baxter Junior in the theatre!" Baer wheezed, "as if!"

Paul and I waited.

"So?" I asked.

"Unlike yours truly," Erica answered, "he did not inherit Pop's drive to succeed. He runs children's parties in Litchfield."

People walking by on Tenth Street heard their roars of laughter.

◆◆◆◆◆

On the train back to Hudson, Paul said, "So they were at the theatre but not at the dinner. No help. Still, I'll send someone over to that restaurant and verify their alibi. Is an '82 Folderol an unusual wine?"

"Pomerol."

"Whatever."

"One of the great ones."

"Where is Pomerol?"

"In Bordeaux."

"We're talking French stuff, right?"

"Yes, dear."

"Why don't we get ourselves a bottle of that to drink when we get back from Litchfield tomorrow?"

168

There are several ways to get to Litchfield from Hudson, each more pleasant than the next, especially on a beautiful morning.

Since I was driving, leaving Paul free to mutter orders into the phone and follow up on leads and alibis, I chose the southerly route, cutting across Columbia County through Millerton (stop at Harney's for a pot of Paris tea if you are not in the middle of a murder inquiry), then head toward Sharon, on through Cornwall, turn right at Goshen, and you'll shortly be cruising into Litchfield which looks the way America is supposed to look. Broad swaths of green on either side of the road flanked by excellent specimens of colonial architecture, gracious houses with elegant proportions and beautifully manicured lawns and gardens.

Litchfield has a bit of history we wouldn't want to overlook.

Beginning in 1784, a Litchfield lawyer, the smartly-named Tapping Reeve, opened Litchfield Law School, the first law school in the young United States. He wrote a series of formalized lectures codifying legal precepts to insure all students had access to the same body of knowledge. Vice Presidents Aaron Burr and John C. Calhoun, over one hundred members of the United States House of Representatives, numerous United States senators, United States cabinet secretaries, justices of the United States Supreme Court, state governors, and state supreme court chief justices all attended Litchfield Law.

In 1792, Sarah Pierce established Litchfield Female Academy as one of the first major educational institutions for women in the United States.

The famous Beechers, an illustrious family of educators and abolitionists including Harriet Beecher Stowe, Henry Ward Beecher, and Charles Beecher, all grew up in Litchfield.

During the early years of the 19th century, Litchfield's fortunes declined. Lacking an adequate water supply for industry and having no rail transportation, the village became a rural backwater. Rediscovered as a resort community in the late 19th and early 20th century, Litchfield became a popular spot for vacation, weekend, and summer homes. The town embraced the Colonial Revival movement, and by the early 20th century most of the homes, especially on the broad, tree-lined parkways through the center of town, began to sport the white paint and black shutters seen today.

The town's pristine architecture transports one back to the Colonial era.

Among the Main Street storefronts, Cassandra's stepson combined his business and residence in a loft space above a women's clothing store which I felt sure still had some Villager blouses and Pappagallos in its stockroom. We rang the buzzer and the intercom voice replied, "Yes?" to which Paul replied, "Sheriff here, Mr. Baxter."

A large man with a broad, cheerful face opened the door. He wore a red plaid shirt and fatigue pants over Army boots.

After introductions, we were invited upstairs.

"So you do children's parties?" Paul began.

"What? Where'd you get that, haven't done those in years. Oh, wait!" He grinned. "From my charming sister, I'll bet."

He shook his head. "Not so many children's parties anymore. That was when I was much, much younger, although I still do it occasionally. Just between us, I've always been a sucker for birthday cake! But now most of my work is for corporate clients. Corporate training. Corporate off-sites."

"What do you do for the companies?" I asked.

"Usually sales meetings, motivational stuff. Role playing, how not to make a sales call, giving exceptional performers some recognition among their peers, that sort of thing. We put on shows!"

"All the way out here?" Paul asked. "Looks like there wouldn't be enough work."

"There's sort of a circuit, lots of companies in Hartford, Stamford, Boston. And I work in Manhattan a good deal. Here, let me show you."

Opening his laptop, he showed us several photographs and videos. He appeared as a clown, as a pirate, a caveman---any number of disguises---as well as in business suits role-playing with men and women also in business suits.

"Who are all these people in costume?" I asked during one video, a very slickly produced piece of musical comedy that wouldn't have been out of place on a legitimate stage---except it was promoting ad sales for a leading broadcast network.

"Ah, yes! Our merry troupe! Somewhere between burlesque and Gilbert & Sullivan! We highlight corporate meetings, incentive award programs. We write songs, dance, do sketches, whatever the client needs. But! Songs and skits with a purpose! Entertain and flatter the employees! Motivate the lads and lasses on the sales teams! Instill the old esprit right in the heart of the corps! Doing our bit for the economy, you might say. It also pays very well and the work is steady."

He closed the laptop.

"So one could say that you are in show business, like your sister---and your late stepmother." My observation was not well received.

"The less said about my 'family,' the better," he snorted.

"My sister couldn't act her way out of a paper bag. Her entire oeuvre could be called the menopause chronicles. She is permanently wistful, stuck in---no, not a rut---but a chasm of mediocrity, born to banality. A Hilary Swank for the ages. At least *I'm* not deluding myself about *my* talent."

"Such a close family!" I opined. "Do you have any kind words about your late stepmother, Cassandra?"

171

"The kindest thing I can say is that despite her obvious avarice, she did make my father happy in the last twenty years of his life. There are far too many critical, mean things one could say, all negative energy, all pointless. Dad made his money and he was entitled to spend it any way he wanted as far as I'm concerned. Erica insisted he had some paternal obligation to share the wealth with us, but I never agreed.

"I perform, I have a good time, make a good living. And, I've made my own way, just as my father did." He paused.

"Your coming out here to see me---well, I gather the old girl did not just keel over, which was the impression I got from the obit in the *Times*. And because Erica and I will inherit something, not at all clear how much, that puts us on your radar as 'persons of interest.' "

Paul nodded. "That's about right," he said.

Baxter grinned. " 'Persons of interest.' Wonder if I can work that into a show? Jargon is everything!"

Paul asked, "We need to eliminate you from the inquiry, Mr. Baxter. Where were you on the Saturday evening Cassandra Chappelle died?"

"I was pulling rabbits out of a hat and making things disappear!"

"What?" Paul and I asked in unison.

"Magic started as a hobby when I was a kid. Actually, I got into it because of Dad. He loved to do card tricks and impromptus and he wasn't half bad! He taught me some and I kept at it until I got pretty proficient. I do all sorts of illusions, sleight of hand. I'm a member of the American Society and also the Magic Circle in London. At *their* annual meeting last year, Prince Charles performed right after I did! Anyhow, my lady friend runs the Litchfield historical society up here. Their summer benefit was last Saturday. I worked it.

"I spent the early part of the evening going from table to table, doing card tricks, finding live birds in men's pockets,

172

pulling eggs out of women's ears, or a $1000 bill out of a kid's nose. A great evening! At the end, they auctioned a one-hour private performance by me at the winning bidder's home. Some gal paid $10,000 for my talents after I had stumped her on the cups and balls routine half a dozen times!

"So that's where I was, from 5 o'clock or so until almost 11pm."

I hesitated for about a nanosecond but then blurted out, "Would you do that one for us?"

Baxter grinned broadly. "Cups and balls? Delighted!"

Reaching into a drawer in his desk he extracted three red balls and three small silver cups. He pulled a small side table over between us.

Expertly maneuvering his props between his hands and the tabletop, he said, "This is a very old trick. Romans performed it two thousand years ago, as well as the Egyptians, the Chinese, the Indians. Also very popular in the Middle Ages. It's an ancient routine with many, many variations. Sheriff, where am I putting the ball?"

"Under the middle cup," Paul said confidently. "In the city, they do this as Three Card Monte," he added.

"Are you suggesting stakes, Sheriff?" Baxter asked casually.

"How about a dollar?" said the big spender with the badge.

"A dollar it is!" Baxter cried and deftly manipulated the cups, raising each one occasionally to show where the ball had landed. Moving them around a few more times on the table, he looked up at Paul.

"And the ball is...where, Sheriff?"

I thought it was in the center and that's the one Paul pointed to.

But no! It was on the right end. Baxter did the trick six more times. By turns, the single ball vanished, three balls appeared, then all three vanished, one invariably turned up where we had not expected and finally transformed into a radish, then a shiny green glass marble, then a ping-pong ball. Paul gave up and reached for his wallet in a state of astonishment.

Baxter waved him off, saying, "Don't be silly, Sheriff! This was all in fun. I wish I'd known you were interested in magic, I'd have been more prepared...I can also do this trick using baby chicks!"

◆◆◆◆◆

As we drove home, Paul said, "That guy is ruled out, right?"

"I would say yes, unless his illusory excellence makes it magically possible for him to be in two places at once."

"I'm glad," Paul said, fiddling with the radio until he found an oldies station. "I liked him. We've got too damned many suspects anyway. Course, I'll still have his alibi checked out. Wish I could have seen him find a $1000 bill."

"In case you are interested, I'm very good at making those *disappear,*" I said.

"I'll just bet you are," he laughed.

"Are you in the mood for a slight detour?" Paul asked hopefully.

"Your command is my wish, dear. Where to?"

"I could use a good cup of coffee. They have that nice place in Rhinebeck..."

"For that matter," I said, "we'll be going through Millerton in a few minutes. Why not stop for a cuppa at Irving Farm?" A nifty little spot in the center of town.

"That would not further our investigation!" Paul said gruffly.

Paul added, as he sometimes does, that he had a 'fifth sense' about 'those Tenth Street idiots.' Ignoring my usual response of, 'Really? Is it sight? Is it smell?' he said, "I want to get coffee at that place the daughter and son-in-law say they had dinner the night Cassandra was poisoned. We'll personally check out Trenton/Baer's alibi."

Not quite an hour later, we were rolling into Rhinebeck.

174

Other than the traffic light at the main intersection, indeed, the only traffic light in town, which is so ineffectually regulated it would try the patience of Job, Rhinebeck is exceedingly pleasant. Not as large as Hudson's burgeoning Warren Street, Rhinebeck's downtown is a sedate array of interesting restaurants and shops, anchored at the main intersection---where the red and green signals exist in their own, separate universe---by the Beekman Arms, Foster's Tavern, the Rhinebeck Department Store, and, until recently, a tobacconist complete with wooden Indian on the sidewalk, representing a Sepasco chief in full dress attire, complete with headdress.

I'm going to miss that guy.

The Rhinebeck Department Store is in a very handsome Italian Renaissance Revival three-storey brick building which has been a cornerstone of Rhinebeck since 1890. The store is an excellent pre- or post-lunch destination if you wish to be transported back to an era when sales people were helpful, and well-made, comfortable, traditional sportswear was the rule rather than the exception. The merchandise selection is pitch-perfect for the country squire or squirette, whether you are looking for a Pendleton shirt in the fall, a sporty golf ensemble in the spring, or the perfect cords or chinos. I defy you to get in and out without buying a sweater---I know I've never been able to.

Foster's Coach House Tavern, also built circa 1890, has long been a favorite of Bennett's and mine, with its definitive turkey sandwich, excellent draft beer, and comely staff. We always choose the horse tack bedecked barroom for our luncheons, especially on fall weekends so we can catch a football game on the flat screen hanging behind the bar between the gins and the ryes. I explain the strategies of the split T-formation, the draw, the quarterback sneak, the reverse, the option, et alia, to Bennett. When we are in England, he explains cricket to me.

Utterly unfathomable.

Across the street, the Beekman Arms, the oldest Inn in America, began in 1704 when one William Traphagen established a traveler's inn, the Traphagen Tavern, at the town crossroads. Colonized since the 1680s by the Dutch, back then Ryn Beck---a portmanteau word combining the name of the town's founder, Wilhelmus Beekman, and his native Netherlands home, Rhineland--- was a small settlement carved out of forests inhabited by Sepasco indians. Next to the inn, the King's Highway, now known as Route 9, intersects the Sepasco Trail, now Market Street, which meanders down to the Hudson River. The Beekman Arms--- named after the Beekman family, prominent original British Crown land owners in the Hudson Valley---was added to that original tavern in 1766 and has been operating ever since.

Bogardus Tavern, as the formidable timber and stone building was known during the last third of the 18th century, played a role in the American Revolution. The Continental Army's Fourth Regiment drilled on the front lawn and the tavern also sheltered patriots during the war. When the British burned the colonial state capital, Kingston, across the river, townsfolk took refuge in the inn. George Washington, Philip Schuyler, Benedict Arnold, and Alexander Hamilton all slept, ate, drank, argued, and caroused here throughout the Revolutionary War.

In 1804, after Jefferson shunned his then vice-president from the national ticket, Aaron Burr entered an intense race for the governorship of New York. Hamilton was publicly critical of Burr. In late June, amid the bitterly contested campaign, General Alexander Hamilton and Colonel Aaron Burr quarreled fiercely in the Beekman Inn's tavern. Their dispute culminated in a duel.

Today, the Beekman Arms does a brisk business as a hostelry and in its low-ceilinged tavern and airier dining rooms and sunporch. The original guest registry lists prices from the 18th century---how much for boarding your horse and his hay, or housing your carriage, or providing room and board for yourself and your servants. A later registry bears the signatures of more

176

recent notables who have stayed at the Beekman. Let me toss out a few names---Livingston, Rockefeller, Astor, Cronkite, Brinkley, Winfrey, Clinton, Gore, Taylor, Vidal, Midler, Lansbury, Newman, Nicholson, Pfeiffer, Kidman, Louis-Dreyfus, Bacall, and Ono. Everyone likes to savor genuine Americana---and the Beekman Arms is the real deal.

Our destination, Le Petit Bistro, is a charming storefront restaurant recently expanded to include the Indian chief's former space. They opened shortly after I arrived in the Valley and were in the vanguard of farm-to-table, foraged and local produce, artfully prepared fresh steaks, seafood, and classic dishes. I love the place and felt hungry as we walked in at about 4 o'clock.

There were three or four tables of late lunchers and a couple of folks having wine at the bar. A maitre d' welcomed us. "Table for two?" he smiled.

Paul said, "No, thanks. We'll just perch at the bar." As we were being shown to our seats, opposite the snug, pine-paneled dining room, Paul showed his badge.

"We're here to follow up on a couple who had dinner with you last Saturday night. Who would know about that? Who would have waited on them?"

The maitre d' answered, "Let me see. I'm not really certain about which staff worked Saturday but I can check. You say they were here for dinner?"

Paul nodded.

"In the meantime, what may I bring you?" He gave us two menus.

I spoke up and said, "May we see a wine list?"

The maitre d' smiled and said, "Oui, madame, right away."

The wine list appeared. No Pomerol.

A waiter came up to us and said, "I worked last Saturday night. How can I help?"

Paul produced photos of Trenton and Baer. "Did you wait on these people?"

The waiter studied the photos, scratched his chin and said, "I seated them about 4 o'clock, maybe 4.30. That's when I went off duty. That's a slow time of day."

Paul asked, "So you don't know what time they left?"

"Sorry, no. I left right after they were seated."

"Could you check your credit card payments that night?"

The waiter shook his head. "You'd have to get the owner to do that. Sorry."

Paul said, "OK, thanks. We'll be in touch."

Paul took my elbow and eased me off the stool as my stomach kept growling. Heading out the door he said, "Don't worry. I'm feeding you over to the Beekman. Call that guy Baer and ask him about the wine. Maybe you can rattle him."

I dialed Baer in the Village and when he answered, I said, "Lindsey Brooks here. The sheriff and I were just at Petit Bistro. There's no '82 Pomerol on their wine list. Do you want to modify what you told us you were doing for dinner Saturday night?"

"Dear me!" cried Baer. "Sorry for the confusion. I brought the wine from home, just paid corkage. If you'll reread our statement, you'll see I said 'we *drank* a Pomerol,' not that we *bought* the bottle."

Paul did not receive that news well. Exasperated after a long day, we both ordered beers and burgers in the Beekman tavern with its scant seven foot ceilings and forest of Windsor chairs.

Perhaps to put some distance between us and our fruitless day, Paul asked, "Did you know that FDR began every one of his four presidential campaigns in front of the Beekman?"

PAUL DECIDES TO ARREST FRANCESCA

When we reconvened at the incident room, Paul was not jolly.

"Lindsey, I have to tell you as a professional courtesy. It looks like we are going to have to bring in Francesca O'Connell. We are also bringing in Ben Barrow. There's just too much to ignore."

At my pained expression, Paul said, "Yes, I know a lot of it is circumstantial. They are both going to get a polygraph test."

"Those aren't admissible."

"No, but they may help us get some answers."

"Paul, it is *all* circumstantial."

"At this moment it is. Yes and no. Means, motive, and opportunity. We are doing a computer enhancement of the video tape. Five bucks says the guy on it is Barrow.

"I'm bringing them in. It's time to throw Mrs. O'Connell under the elephant in the room."

Conversation with Francesca

I opened the O'Connells' front door, calling out, "Hi, Mom, I'm home!" as usual.

Francesca called back to me, "Dining room!"

She was at the dining table, a big piece, easily seats twenty. Deep mahogany sheen. Regency revival chairs with gilded sphinxes on the arms done in an Italian wine and lemon striped velvet. A magnificent room with the Lucian Freud hanging above the mantle. Francesca, a very pale, and I thought, frail figure, sat alone. I joined her.

"Lindsey, Franklin told me you called him. That you said I needed to get an attorney. This can't be true. You know very well I had nothing to do with that women's death. Don't you? Don't you? And why does that damned sheriff keep banging on about the salad! There is no PROOF the poison was even in the salad! Is there?"

"Francesca, I believe you. To me it simply looks like circumstantial evidence. But still, there's a hell of a lot of it."

After a deep breath, I asked, "Did you know that Franklin and Cassandra had been lovers many years ago?"

"*Now* I fucking do! He *finally* managed to tell me last night. *So what already?!* Look, maybe he *did* look back on their romance through his rose-tinted tri-focals. Maybe he *was* fond of her, young love and all that crap. But he would *never* leave me. I'm his life. I'm his partner. The first time we went out was to some sort of dopey African travelogue at St. Bart's church. He walked me home, came up for a night cap, *and never left*. Our life together has been perfect from Day One. That woman was no threat to me.

"And another thing? Why doesn't your brilliant pal the sheriff go after her damn stepchildren? *They're* the ones who have a real motive---HER MONEY!! They would have inherited the rest of their dad's estate when she popped, right?"

"Yes, they were in line to inherit. But they weren't in a position to put the poison in her salad."

"How do you know that?"

"Francesca, they weren't at your dinner before the theatre."

"*The hell they weren't!* I talked to them myself! I recognized her from her movies---in fact, at one point, there was quite a little love fest of her menopausal fans, all thrilled to meet Erica Trenton. Of course, her husband, David Baer, the playwright, is the *real* talent. I talked to *him*."

This was major news. They were there.

"Where were they and this crowd of people? Why didn't I see them?"

"At the far, far end of the living room, down by the piano. I don't know where you were. You probably never got that far from the bar. But there were swarms of people all over the house, like two hundred and eleven, I can believe you missed them. And also, they were last-minute adds---so even at dinner you wouldn't have seen them because we had to seat them in Siberia---behind a column in the foyer outside the main room where you were seated. No wonder you didn't see them. Wait! You probably didn't even know them, did you? How *could* you have recognized them?"

"No, actually I didn't." Another good point.

"Who arranged for them to come?"

"That drama teacher, the guy directing the play. What's his name? He was here that night just for drinks, I think. Palmer, that's it. Said he was calling for Jason, asked if I could please add them, said they were writing a big check to the drama department."

181

"Paul, new development!" I yelled into my phone.

"Make this quick, I'm waiting on my warrant for Mrs. O'Connell."

"You might want to wait until you have had another talk with Baxter's children."

"The actress and her wino husband? Mr. Folderol? What's new about them?"

"Surprise! They must have had a *very* early dinner in Rhinebeck because they were also at the O'Connells' dinner that night. *They were there!* And *they lied* about it."

"How do you know that? Who told you they were there?" Paul thundered.

"Francesca."

Paul was furious. "You must be effing kidding me! You warned her about the arrest warrant! Did you suggest she might want to get her plane fueled up and file a flight plan for Acapulco? No, wait! We have an extradition treaty with Mexico. Where else? Where would she go? Where did you suggest?! Damn it, Lindsey! Damn it!"

"Don't be mad at me! I just wanted to make sure she'd been in touch with her lawyer! She's not going to run. She has to think of Franklin's business. She's not going to act like she's guilty when she isn't. Those two people were there. *And they lied about it!*"

"I see your point." He sounded calmer. "I'll bring them in. And I'll hold off on her warrant. Good work, Lindsey."

"One more thing," I said. "Not Mexico. Mustique."

PAUL BRINGS IN BAXTER'S KIDS

Because of Paul's illustrious earlier career with the NYPD, he is able to pull a few strings when he needs to.

The first string he pulled this afternoon produced a squad car with two uniforms and a captain appearing at the door of the Tenth Street apartment and suggesting to Erica Trenton and David Baer that they were invited in for further questioning on the murder of their stepmother. Would they come voluntarily? They would.

The second string he pulled produced a Sikorsky helicopter at the Chelsea heliport into which the Trenton-Baers were bundled. Slightly over an hour later, they were walking into an interrogation room in Paul's Hudson office.

Voluntarily, but still, less than happy campers.

Designated The Good Cop, I walked in first and took coffee orders.

Coffee delivered, now it was the sheriff's turn to make his entrance and deliver his dramatic opening line: "What have we here? The Pinocchio Twins! You have any new lies to tell us?" Paul swiveled a chair around and straddled it in front of them.

"Don't be funny!" Erica Trenton shrilled. "You've got a damned nerve hauling us up here. Why didn't *you* come to us like before? I've got a good mind to call our attorney!" She wanted to sound angry but came across as panicky, I thought.

David Baer echoed those sentiments. "I was going to call our attorney an hour ago but it was so damned loud in the helicopter, I could hardly hear myself think. Would you mind telling us what this is all about?"

"Same as last time---it's about Cass Chappelle's death. Only now we have something new. You have been placed at the scene of the crime."

"What crime? Of course we saw her die, *just like everyone else in the theatre*! Are you planning to arrest us? Then you'll have to arrest the entire audience!" Ms. Trenton's voice had gone up an octave.

Paul glanced at me.

I said, "Oh, my, no. That's *not* the scene of the crime. The crime was committed at the O'Connells' house..."

"Where you both were!" Paul thundered.

"Yes, you were at Petit Bistro and they remembered the wine you ordered---no, sorry, *drank*. But you had no reservation, the maitre d' wasn't entirely certain about what time you came in, or more pertinently, *left the restaurant*, since the restaurant had a shift change in the late afternoon, but it was not sure as hell not in the evening. Francesca O'Connell says you were at her party throughout cocktails and dinner and *that* is when the woman was poisoned."

"Poisoned? Cass was poisoned? How do you know that?" Baer looked personally insulted.

"We know that because Frank Carver's mommy and daddy spent a fortune for him to go to the University of Pennsylvania medical school so he could live in Hudson, New York and be my god-damned medical examiner. That's how we know it. And that is how we know about the other dead guy you probably also killed. This friends, is what we call 'probable cause'.

"And this," he said, waving a few stapled sheets of paper, "is what we call a search warrant for your computers. We'll pick those up at the same time we take you home. Which is now. Sgt. Jackson, you and Sgt. O'Reilly escort these two back to the copter. When you get to their residence in New York, pick up their computers, phones, tablets, anything that sends and receives. And people, make sure the sergeant has *everything*. And at your Connecticut residence, and whatever offices you may have, make the sergeants aware as we need the electronics from there, as well. You don't want to be in any more trouble than you are in right now. Understood?"

They nodded. Difficult to imagine two more miserable-looking specimens.

"Good. Lindsey, come with me."

After their exit, Paul said, "NYPD will have two unmarked cars outside their apartment 24/7. We'll put a tail on them whenever they leave their house. Damn it, Lindsey, I feel like we might finally be getting somewhere. But I want all the info I can possibly pull together before we put them into full interrogation."

"There is one other thing, of course," I said. "We not only didn't know they were at the dinner that night, none of us could *identify* them at that point, and none of us has any idea whether they were in full view of others for the entire evening."

Paul smiled. "See? I knew you could be useful! I guess Mrs. O'Connell is going to have to give us a list of the folks they sat with and we're going to have to get better acquainted with Erica Trenton and David Baer's fan club.

"Organize that, Lindsey."

LISTS IN THE INCIDENT ROOM

It was a beautiful, sunny day, perfect for a stroll to clear my head before convening in the incident room.

I walked south off-campus toward the center of Annandale, past the pretty gray and white Gothic revival Episcopal Church. In the center of what was the village square in earlier times, I circled the gazebo, preserved as lovingly as a Revolutionary War relic. Inside the gazebo is an old-fashioned pump with its handle missing. Bard alums say it was the inspiration for a line in Bob Dylan's 'Subterranean Homesick Blues': 'The pump don't work 'cause the vandals took the handle.'

I strolled back to the small cottage, sat down and put my feet up on my desk. Sunlight filtered in through the windows as I looked out into the woods that surround the house on three sides. Look at those pretty little wild violets and ostrich ferns! What lovely trees, I thought. Birch, locust, oak. Two squirrels were exercising their Wallenda genes, leaping from branch to branch, from maple to hickory, scarcely pausing for footing before they set off again, darting and jumping. What a perfect day to pack a picnic, stroll over to Blithewood, the old mansion, and recline in the garden while gazing at the river, munching on paté and deviled eggs, sipping Champagne.

Or not, quoth Reality.

"Listen up, team!"

The sheriff had arrived.

Paul stood with one hand on his hip, studying photos, maps, notes, and connecting arrows that covered the walls, and slapping the side of his leg with the yardstick in his other hand.

"'This is a damned hodge-podge!"

He gestured threateningly with the yardstick at the evidence pinned and taped to the south wall. "We've got to put some order on to it. Lindsey, let's rank order our suspects. Jackson, get up here and make a new chart."

Jackson grabbed a clean white board and a marker and prepared to take notes.

Paul continued, "We got two murders."

"Excuse me, sir. Don't we have three? The man in the boathouse?" asked Jackson.

"Yes, that's true, damn it!" Paul answered. "However, at the moment, we believe the chef was killed only to facilitate the poison being delivered to the Chappelle woman. Let's keep him in mind, but I want us to focus on Chappelle and Brad Ruffin, understood?"

Paul walked over to the incident board and pointed to the photograph of Cassandra lying dead in the aisle at the theatre.

"Let's consider Cass Chappelle first. She was after Franklin O'Connell. That is the only relevant fact. And, therefore, Francesca O'Connell is first in line as a suspect."

"Wait! Wait!" I cried. "What about that Cass was also seeing Brad? She was apparently a mentor, coaching him as an actor. She may even have offered to stake him to a move to New York. And may have even been romantically involved," I added.

"Are you saying the boy somehow poisoned her?" Paul screwed up his most skeptical face. "If she was buttering his bread, why would he? And how could he? And while I'm at it on your hare-brained theories, how could they possibly be romantically involved?! Very doubtful. Sure, she may have encouraged his interest but..."

"No, I am suggesting that maybe someone wanted to break the hold she had on the boy. Permanently."

Paul answered, "OK, whatever, fine. Still, that person *must have been* at the dinner."

187

I countered with, "Why is Francesca your primary suspect? What about Baxter's kids? Who lied to us! They're the ones who stand to gain the most. Why aren't they on the top of your list?"

Paul asked, "Did they strike you as being desperate for money? They own a town house in the Village, they have a country place in Roxbury. His plays are performed someplace every year, doesn't that make lots of money? What does she get to do a film?"

I answered, "I recall reading somewhere that the average successful playwright makes $25,000 to $50,000 in royalties a year. Property taxes on their city house would eat that and Roxbury is not cheap either. She might get $500,000 or a million for a film but she doesn't work much. So maybe they did need some new money."

Paul said, "OK! So they could have been serious about getting Chappelle's money. But we don't even know how much money there is! Who else was at the dinner?"

O'Reilly answered. "What about the dead kid's parents? They were there. Maybe Ruffin killed her to generate bad publicity for O'Connells' companies. He stiffed him a long time ago on those mineral deposits. Very bad feelings."

"Whoever killed the chef. That's the guy," I said. "Find out who bought the knock-out spray."

"Now let's take a look at Murder #2. Brad Ruffin. Why kill him?" Paul asked.

"I don't see any motive," I said. "Obviously, there was one. But what and for whom? He was a college kid."

"The angry girlfriend is probably our best shot. She said he was leaving her. Would have made her mad," Sgt. O'Reilly said and Jackson nodded.

"And she was on stage. Palmer was on stage, too. Has to be one of them."

"We still haven't found the murder weapon. That would help," opined Jackson.

Paul was shifting into an even higher gear.

"Come here, you two. I've got some stuff for you to follow up on. Same as with those Tenth Street idiots. I want every phone, every computer, every tablet, every electronic anything that belongs to every one of these people, I want it pulled in and taken apart. I want all phone records, all texts, all email looked at. Go and get your search warrants now!"

"Sir," Jackson spoke up. "We can get the warrants and bring the stuff in but we don't have anyone who knows how to, well, take them apart, as you put it. Run checks on things. Override their passwords." He looked gloomy.

"I know someone who'd work," I volunteered. "Nice, bright neighborhood kid. He used to mow my grass. Now he's a hot shot programmer and analyst. Ryan Herbert. He could do the computer investigation work you need."

"Get him in here!" Paul yelled.

A few hours later, after meeting with his boss and explaining that Law Enforcement needed professional technical assistance, Jackson and O'Reilly ushered Ryan Herbert into the office.

Ryan is a rather hefty but handsome thirty-something lad with red-gold hair and a beard to match, wearing no-frame glasses, a purple polo shirt, and bright green chinos.

Paul began by telling him the scope of the job.

"This is a triple murder investigation and we've got several suspects," Paul said. "Each one has a computer, a laptop, a phone or two, probably some Facebook accounts, and on-line purchases. We want to know if they talked to each other or if they had any interaction with our three dead people, Cassandra Chappelle, Brad Ruffin, and the CIA chef, Perry Burr. How long will that take?"

Ryan chortled. "Since you told my boss when you commandeered me for this project that you'd need me for a week, I guess it will take a week. It would be easier to estimate if I actually had any of the devices in my hands."

On cue, the deputies strode in carrying laptops, phones, and tablets. They put the electronics in piles across two long tables. Each was labeled with the owner's name.

"First, here's the stuff that belonged to the dead people. And over here, here's Palmer, the roommate Eli Johnson, and Francesca O'Connell's stuff. The Ruffin's laptops and tablets are being brought in from the city and Connecticut and will be here later tonight along with their phones. Where do you want him to start?" they asked Paul.

"Start with the dead people," Paul snapped.

"If I may add just one thing," I interjected. "The knock-out spray is a big link we don't have yet. Someone probably bought that on-line. When we know who did, we know who killed Cassandra."

"You can find that, right?" Paul asked, placing a firm hand on Ryan's shoulder.

"That kind of depends, sir," Ryan answered. "Web browsers can store cookies and cache web pages. They can show when and where something was searched, viewed, and purchased and by whom. The variables we have to deal with are the websites visited and the settings in the web browsers. Those settings might not allow stored cookies or cached pages. They also might have an expiration threshold that limits how long the data is stored. Also if someone revisits the same site it could over-write existing data stored thus eliminating your earlier tracks."

"Well, start," Paul said. "And as for you, Lindsey, get back over to the O'Connells'. Get me that list!"

Turning to his deputies, he said sharply, "And you two. Check out who sat with the Ruffins, at the dinner and at the

190

theatre. Check out who sat next to Cassandra at the dinner that night. Go talk to her housekeeper. Find out if she ate anything before she went to the O'Connells' party. We're missing some connection between the forest and the trees."

FRANCESCA TALKS SEATING ARRANGEMENTS

"I can hardly believe I have the pleasure of your frigging company again!"

Francesca was sitting in Franklin's office, a tweed and tartan snuggery, with book-lined walls, deep green draperies, and photographs of his Bugatti, his Isotta-Fraschini, and his Hispano Suiza at car shows in Monte Carlo and the Villa d'Este on Lake Como. Another showed Franklin and Francesca embracing on the hood of a 1951 Maserati after he won the Goodwood Revival outside Chichester, England a few years ago.

Between the two French windows hung two small paintings from Franklin's collection which I have admired for years: A small Alan Davie, a variation of 'Bird Noises,' and an R.B. Kitaj of a dancing nude wearing an orange turban and orange boa while brandishing a cigarette holder.

"When you called, you said that the sheriff needs my help," Francesca said tersely. "And I need a loggia on the Grand Canal. Which do you think is my priority?"

A distinctly chilly Francescan tone.

"May I remind you that you are not out of the woods yet?" I snapped, taking a chair beside her.

"To date, every damned scrap of circumstantial evidence in Cassandra's murder points to you and your staff. Further, you will be fascinated to hear that a *Wall Street Journal* reporter is taking me to breakfast tomorrow. He's absolutely wild to know more about how you and your husband, Mr. Rare Earth, aka Señor Solar, aka Frankie the Tidal Titan, fit into this sordid little story." A white lie but I hoped a useful one.

"Is this blackmail?!" she fumed.

"No, it is not blackmail. It is a great opportunity for you to help us identify the actual killers. Doesn't that seem like a good use of time?"

"What sort of help?"

"You've already scored big by pointing out that Erica Trenton and David Baer were at the dinner, which we did not realize since they made a point of saying they were not. That may have been a big break---they had a hell of a lot to gain by her death---and we have you to thank. Now I need names, dear, names of the people who were seated with Erica Trenton and David Baer at dinner as well as those with whom they schmoozed during the cocktail hour. Would you please toddle off and find those seating charts?"

While Francesca went to collect her file on the party I texted Paul to say we were making progress and ask when he wanted to meet these people. We agreed to interview them en masse.

Francesca reappeared with her laptop, sat down at Franklin's desk, and began to review the charts.

"Here you go. Let me bring these up and send them to you."

Eight guests shared a table with Trent and Baer the evening of the party, four of whom also heavily mingled with them during most of the cocktail hour. Francesca emailed the names and contact info to Paul's office; a date to gather these folks together was set for Saturday morning.

At that moment, two golden labs raced around the corner barking, closely followed by Franklin, wearing grease-stained overalls and a Yankees cap.

"What are you two wanton women doing in my man cave!?" he shouted before enveloping his wife in his arms for a major smooch and following up by giving me a hug and a kiss on each cheek.

"I've got an appointment," said Francesca. "SO GLAD to have been of help! Do let me know if I can be of further assistance," she snarled with a fake smile as she stalked out and slammed the door.

"I'd best be on my way, as well," I said, leaping up.

"Not so fast, young lady. Sit back down," Franklin ordered.

"You and I have some unfinished business. Would you like to bring me up to date on the investigation? Francesca said your pal the sheriff is so close to arresting her that she made me call our lawyer. You don't honestly think Francesca would have killed anyone, do you?" Franklin looked very anxious.

"Your opinion would be more interesting than mine, no?"

"You'd be right in saying she was pissed. I was behaving like a complete idiot, an utter fool. Francesca is everything to me. I wouldn't be the success I am today without her confidence and support. I'd have made the money but I wouldn't be a *success*--- she's given me a life, she's steered me into philanthropy, she's my inspiration."

Since I could not---quite yet---honestly agree with him on Francesca's innocence, I changed the subject.

"When did you get the Kitaj and the Davie?" I asked. "They are so fabulous."

"Long ago, late sixties, I think. The Davie in Crete when I was on leave. I met him one night while he was playing clarinet with some pick-up jazz group. I bought it off the wall of the bar. The Kitaj a few years later when he was just starting out. I was stationed at a US-UK surveillance station in Cornwall and got a weekend pass to go up to London. He was teaching at Ealing and showing in a little gallery in Charing Cross. Hadn't gotten much attention yet. Luck's usually on my side, at least with art work. But I could use some luck lately. This case is killing me. It's killing both of us."

He wiped his face and eyes with a bandanna from his pocket as he sat down heavily next to me.

"Lindsey, let's make a deal. I'll gladly give you both these paintings if you'll just find the guy who actually murdered those people and let my wife alone. She seems indestructible but this is driving both of us crazy. Half the time, Francesca is in tears or won't even leave her room. I've tried to get it out of my mind but I can't even concentrate on changing sparkplugs. We're both shattered that something so terrible could have happened right in our house. In our own house, for God's sake.

"What were you two talking about? Any good news?"

"Maybe. Cassandra's stepkids were at your party that night. They lied to us, said they weren't. In theory, that gave them the opportunity to poison Cassandra. We're going to talk to the people who were at their table and also at drinks. It's a new lead we got from Francesca. They might be our new best bets."

Franklin brightened slightly.

"God, I hope so. Keep me posted. Find the bastard who did this. Clear our good name. Give me back the wife I love. And remember what I said, Lindsey. Those paintings would look great in your house."

"How about throwing in the Maserati?" I said and ran.

DINNER GUESTS AND SCHMOOZERS

Paul decided the witnesses who had dined with Trent and Baer would be more relaxed and forthcoming if we interviewed them over drinks on my porch. His deputies would get certain particulars beforehand, then the questions would come from me and Paul. We had a gorgeous summer evening and Bennett had prepared a delicious array of hors d'oeuvres, an extravagant departure from our usual rule of Only Nuts.

First to arrive at six sharp were Eleanor Andrews and husband William. In their late fifties and retired from advertising. House in Rhinebeck.

Gina Wolfe, an attorney in Red Hook, and her date for that evening at the O'Connells', Steve Pollard, a psychiatrist in Rhinebeck. Both were in their forties.

Two men, Terrence Stratford and Hugh Austin, were decorators living in Hudson on weekends, Upper East Side in the city. Fiftyish.

Finally, Helene Wharton, a documentary filmmaker and her companion, Bartley Witt, a journalist, who live in Soho in New York City and Chatham up here. Late sixties.

Bennett manned the bar and after everyone was clutching an icy glass of something, I ushered the eight interviewees to the south end of the porch. They arrayed themselves on white Adirondack chairs and a matching settee and on several teak and canvas camp chairs I had nabbed at an auction of a 1920 Bar Harbor estate.

After the murmurs of 'what a lovely view' had subsided, I began by saying, "Thank you all for coming. We are hoping you'll be able to help us get a more complete picture of interactions among guests the night of the party, in particular the movements of two of your dining companions, Erica Trent and David Baer."

"Why is that?" Eleanor Andrews interjected.

"We need to piece together as much information as we can about Cassandra Chappelle's interactions with other people at the party."

"Franklin O'Connell brought Cassandra around to where we were all gathered, in the back of the ballroom, next to the piano. He made introductions, chatted for a bit, then they moved on." This was offered by William Andrews.

"Did Ms. Trent and Mr. Baer speak to Cassandra?" Bennett asked.

"Hmm..." Gina Wolfe spoke up. "You know, I'm not sure Erica was there then. I had been talking to her about how much I love her work, then we decided to go to the powder room. So I wasn't there just then and neither was she, because I only met Cassandra very briefly later in the evening when I went to speak to Franklin just before we sat down for dinner, as I recall."

Hugh Austin said, "I never met the woman. If Franklin brought her around during drinks, Baer was not there and neither were we. Baer had suggested we three take a stroll around the corner of the house to look at the fountains and water garden off the terrace. Terry and I went with him."

"And how was the water garden?" Bennett asked.

"Oh, beautiful lilies! Hyacinth! Golden iris! They even have papyrus! Very attractive!" proclaimed Terrence and Hugh, more or less in unison.

"And how long did you linger by the lilies with the playwright?" I asked.

"Oh, I'd say we were there for perhaps fifteen, maybe twenty minutes. Beautiful spot but there were no waiters circulating back there so we had to go in search of drinks---or rather Baer did. He offered to get our refills."

197

Paul and I looked at each other. `

"That was nice of him. He was gone for, what? A few minutes?" I asked.

"More like ten or even fifteen. Terry and I were walking around, admiring the stone work, the stairs, the landscaping, and chatting with some other guests, so I didn't really notice how long he was away. He did apologize for taking so long, though. Said he had had to run an errand for his wife."

"What was that?" I asked.

"He didn't say."

"But Erica Trent was with you---other than the powder room break?" I asked the women.

Helene Wharton said sharply, "She could hardly get away! We were like a bunch of groupies! Her films have deeply touched the lives of every woman!"

She looked around for corroboration; the other women were nodding, so she continued.

"Especially An Unhinged Spinster! The complexities of marriage, of divorce---and everything in between! Her performance personified the sexual anxieties all women share! Her character asked the eternal question---how will I know when I am happy!?? A tour de force. It was an honor to have those conversations, especially as a filmmaker myself. And now it seems you want us to report on her movements, like spies! I find all of this deeply offensive!" declared Helene Wharton.

Eleanor Andrews spoke up, "May I ask a question?"

"Certainly," I said.

"Did Erica Trent and her husband know Cassandra Chappelle?"

"Yes," I answered. "Erica Trent is, er, was Cassandra's stepdaughter."

"So I gather she would have inherited money when Cassandra Chappelle died?"

"That is correct."

"So what you really want to know is did they have a chance to poison her?"

"Why do you say 'poison'?" Paul asked sharply.

She replied, "My housekeeper's sister is a clerk in the coroner's office. That's what she said. 'Poison.' And she should know, she typed the report."

"I don't know if this helps, but they were both carrying purses," said Steve Pollard.

His companion Gina Wolfe nodded. "Baer was carrying a little reticule and she had an evening bag. Either one of them could have stashed poison in those."

After our guests had left, Paul called Sgt. Jackson telling him to find both purses and get them into forensics to test for traces of aconite.

Refilling his glass, Paul said, "We might be getting someplace. Keep your fingers crossed."

A VISIT TO THE AGENCY AND A CALL TO DOTTIE

The next morning, I took the 8.30am train from Hudson into NYC, then took the Lexington line up to 77th street and walked over to Madison Avenue to the Smythe-Chadwick adoption agency.

The agency had an office in a residential building with the first two floors also housing professional suites. The adoption people kept company with a certified account, a dentist, and an orthopedic surgeon. Love those guys. One-stop shopping.

In nearly all states, records are sealed after an adoption is finalized. Most states have procedures by which parties to an adoption may obtain certain non-identifying information from an adoption record while still protecting the interests of all parties. Police cannot demand records. Courts cannot open records. The state of New York will share the name of the adoption agency---if such exists---and the process takes at least six months.

Basically this means we were looking at a hit or miss situation information-wise but if it was going to be a hit, it would be need to be hitting pretty soon.

My appointment was with the director, a woman of maybe 70-something who was, as my mother would have said, extremely well preserved. She wore a beige and white seersucker shirtwaist dress piped in dark brown with a matching short jacket draped over her shoulders, pearls, and brown and white spectator pumps. The entire effect whispered, *Claire McCardell.*

I, thank God, had also dressed, in a dark navy pant suit, a chartreuse and navy silk print blouse, and pearls, too. My appointment was at 11 o'clock and I arrived at five of.

"Good morning, I'm Lindsey Brooks. Thank you so much for seeing me."

"Good morning, Ms. Brooks. I am Roberta Figgins. Please sit down. How can I help you?"

Sitting across from her immaculate desk, I began.

"What I have is a woman who has been killed. We think her death may have something to do with a son or daughter she gave birth to. The child was likely adopted through this agency. Someone who knew of this child's existence may have seen him or her as a threat, perhaps a threat to a significant inheritance. That is just about the only link we have, and unless you can help me a little bit, we are at a dead end." For an English major, sometimes I don't talk so good.

"Are you a police officer?" Ms. Figgins looked puzzled.

"No. I'm, well, er, no, I'm helping the police on this case but usually I dabble in real estate or buy and sell antiques or I garden."

"Are you a professional gardener?"

"No, but I could be. And it *has* crossed my mind to become one. Plants are definitely so much quieter than people, less disagreeable. Other than aconite, of course." I frowned.

"Have you divided your iris yet this year?" she inquired.

"No. That is on my list very shortly! Do you, uh, need any iris? I have not divided in a few years and I'm afraid we may have a plethora..."

"I would be happy to help you manage your plethora. Nothing is more confounding than an unwanted plethora."

"What a good idea. I'll make a note."

"If you are not a police woman, I fail to see why you are here. Enlighten me?"

"The sheriff in Hudson is an old friend of mine and I've helped him on a few cases involving antiques or art. In this case, he wouldn't even be working on it except the real sheriff in the Rhinebeck jurisdiction had to have emergency back surgery and asked Paul to help out and then Paul, the Hudson sheriff who is helping Hank out, asked me because this involves a lot of weekend people, or prominent people, whom I already know, and I can get people to talk more easily than he can because they know me and I'm so friendly and seem so harmless." I smiled wanly. Think of me as an idiot savant, I prayed.

"It's a little early in the day for a drink, don't you think?" inquired Ms. Figgins.

"What! I haven't been drinking! Oh, I see what you mean! Not necessarily. Heavens, no!"

And so we walked a few blocks down Madison to Bemelman's, the piano bar in the Carlyle Hotel, whose walls consist of murals by Ludwig Bemelman, best known for his illustrations of the Madeline books. Each book begins: 'In an old house in Paris, that was covered with vines, lived twelve little girls in two straight lines... the smallest one was Madeline.'

Daiquiris in hand, we sat at a table just past the end of the bar, the only patrons.

"You surely understand why adoption records are sealed?" Ms. Figgins asked.

"I suppose so. Might be problems otherwise, no?"

"Problems, indeed. Adoption involves remorse of every description. Donors' remorse. Buyers' remorse. Adoptees' remorse. Natural children's remorse. The records must be sealed because otherwise, many adoptions would be revisited *ad infinitum*. Once a decision is made, it cannot be unmade. Naturally, there is a waiting period---usually ninety days---but afterwards, a deal must remain a deal, as it were.

"Tell me the particulars about your case," Ms. Figgins suggested.

"This is---was---a birth mother who would have placed the baby for adoption when he or she was a newborn. As closely as we can calculate, this would have been in the Nineties or so."

"Computers were just coming in then. I am not sure that our records from that period are still in ledgers or if they have been digitized. I have only been here for twenty years. I can check. Was the birth here in New York City? Or did the mother come to us from another town?"

"Our best guess is that the mother lived here and had the baby in a hospital. It was likely a caesarian birth. She would have been older than the average mother, if that helps."

"Was she indigent?"

"Oh, no. Not indigent. In fact, she was a prominent woman of means. Successful. "

"Why was the child placed for adoption?"

"I don't believe the mother's lifestyle would have accommodated an infant."

"Do we know if the father of the child agreed to have it placed for adoption?"

"Not entirely sure who the father might have been."

"I see. All right, do we know who adopted this child?"

"Dorothy and Louis Ruffin."

"I'll see what I can do. Shall we seal the deal?"

"Absolutely."

Calling over to the barkeep, I said, "Jack! May we have two more of those delicious concoctions!"

Ms. Figgins accepted her drink, and said, "Have we had this conversation?"

"Absolutely not, madame. I'll dig the iris. Cheers!"

♦♦♦♦♦

After escorting Ms. Figgins back to her office, I jumped in a cab and hustled down Park Avenue. Dottie had invited me to lunch at her club, the Colony.

The Colony has an excellent buffet and since the only time I usually get there is with my neighbor in the country, maybe once or twice a year, I was very happy to be back, surrounded by the timeless Elsie de Wolfe decor.

Dottie was waiting in the little side parlor on the left when I arrived.

"Hello, dear," I said, giving her a daiquiri-breath peck on the cheek.

Dottie smiled and said, "Have you started without me?"

"Don't get the wrong idea. I had not planned on having anything to drink, much less in broad daylight! My nerves! I went to see the lady at the adoption agency. Drinks were her idea."

Dottie grinned. "Let's get *me* a drink before we start on that saga. Come on."

We got in the elevator and went up to the roof terrace. A nice Jamaican man in a white jacket escorted us to a corner table beneath an umbrella and inquired about beverages.

Dottie said, "Shall we stick with whatever you've been having?"

"Two daiquiris, up," I answered, and after he had left, "the ones at Bemelman's Bar are so tiny. Hardly anything, really. Aren't these pretty little boxwoods!" I said, fondling the leaves.

"Why don't you tell me what's on your mind? You were mysterious on the phone. This is obviously about Brad, no?"

"Dottie, we can't figure out a motive for Brad's death. Most murders are committed for love or money. There is a distinct possibility that his roommate, Eli, killed him, jealous of his leaving her." I left out the part about Louis and the roof.

"I've met Eli. She may be a little mixed up, a little naïve, but she didn't kill Brad. She was in love with him."

"But was he in love with her?" I asked.

She pursed her lips. "Not so sure about that now. I know he was at one point."

"Dottie, if you fell off this terrace, who inherits?"

"Brad *would have* inherited everything. Louis can live on his practice. Brad would have had my family's money."

"Was Louis aware of this?"

"Are you telling me Louis killed Brad?"

"Oh, honestly, I don't know. Somehow, I think the whole thing hinges on who Brad was. Who his birth parents were. Somehow. Who inherits now?"

"I'll give that some thought. I hadn't really considered it. I'll call my attorney. He filed my divorce papers yesterday. I know there are some bequests but the bulk would have gone to Brad, some in trust, some outright.

"Look, I'm still staying at the hotel in Tivoli, I haven't felt like going back to Connecticut. And, in fact, I'm not going anywhere today except to some museums and the ballet. I have to start putting this out of my mind or I will *jump* off this terrace. So why don't you help me? Waiter!"

Lunch ensued with another daiquiri and that sunny terrace pulled us both away from the darkness of the past weeks.

Dropping Dottie at the Met, I caught the 4.30 train back to Hudson.

Bennett met me at the station and hustled me into the car.

"Are we in a rush?" I asked.

Bennett answered, "Slightly, Madame. The sheriff felt you were a little bit the worse for wear and asked me to give you a quiet evening at home."

"Let's go home," I agreed. "We no longer even know what we don't know and I have a headache."

As we drove into the yard, someone who had been sitting on the porch stood, and walked over to wave at us across the railing. It was Eli Johnson.

"I hope you don't mind my making myself at home," she called out.

Bennett and I went in, walked through the house and out onto the porch.

"What an unexpected pleasure," I said. "I'm not sure you and Bennett were properly introduced the other day on the roof. Bennett Holcomb, Eli Johnson. What brings you into our neighborhood?" I smiled, thinking to myself, what in hell are you doing here?

"I have some things I need to tell you, I want to try to explain what's been going on with me," she said.

She and I sat down on a chaise and Bennett sat across from us.

"Brad knew I had slept with his father. He saw the texts from Louis on my phone. He was furious. Called me a lot of really terrible names. Said he'd be glad to see the last of me."

"Were you and Louis a serious item?" I asked. "I mean, were you making plans to be together? Was he leaving his wife?"

She shook her head. "The only reason I went to bed with him was to make Brad jealous. I was confused. I knew Brad was seeing someone else but I didn't know who. And then when he was killed, I felt I was to blame. I just feel so guilty."

"Why would you feel guilty? You didn't kill him---did you, Eli?" I held my breath.

"I don't think so. I don't remember killing him."

"You don't *remember* killing him? What the hell does that mean?"

"I was so upset with him I'd been taking a few sedatives, just to calm down. But I still wanted to punish him. Maybe I wanted him dead so much, it just happened."

"Eli, I think we need to speak to your parents. Would you give me their phone number?"

"I don't know who they are. I grew up in an orphanage."

THE MEDIA APPEARS

As Paul had predicted, the local press had gone berserk about three suspicious deaths in one evening. Following the three-for-the-price-of-one inquest, which returned the verdicts as expected---'suspicious death caused by persons unknown'---Paul prepared to make his remarks outside the courthouse in Dutchess County.

Peeking out from the second story window of the room where we had been assembled for the inquest, I saw about twenty cars and camera vans.

"Paul," I said, slipping my arm around his shoulders, "this news conference is going to put you right up there with Inspector Morse or Lewis. Or that gloomy detective on Broadchurch. I'll be right here behind you." I smiled.

Jason Priestly, whose face betrayed a mood in which he could bite the heads off nails, came up to Paul and said tersely, "I beg you. The lowest ball you can throw. Please. I'm trying to run a school here."

As we quickly walked down the staircase, Paul said, "I'm going to be playing this one a little close to my chest, Lindsey, don't want to give away what we don't know yet."

Ironclad logic, that.

It is not often that a police press conference in the Valley has reporters from the Poughkeepsie *Journal*, The Kingston *Daily Freeman*, The Newburgh *Journal Online*, the Hudson *Register Star*, the Millbrook *Independent*, the Woodstock *Times*, and *Hudson Valley One* as well as the New York City dailies, the *Times*, the *Post*, and the *Daily News*, as well as *The Wall Street Journal.*

I've rarely stood near that many cameras firing away but there is quite a lot of noise as if from very small machine guns. Television video feed operators jostled for position in the glaring sun and a dozen boom mikes swayed and angled toward Paul's head as the sheriff cleared his throat, straightened his tie, and began.

"Good afternoon. I can report that today's inquest, as expected, returned a verdict of three suspicious deaths, all of which occurred in Annandale-on-Hudson. They are: Ms. Cassandra Chappelle, of Rhinebeck and New York, who appeared to have succumbed to a cardiac arrest due to unknown causes while she was a member of the audience in the middle of a theatrical performance at the Bard Theatre. The second, Mr. Bradley Ruffin, a member of the cast at the same performance, appears to have died as a result of injuries sustained on stage. The third, Perry Burr, a faculty member of the Culinary Institute of America, which appears to be a related death, occurred on that Saturday evening as well. Our investigation is on-going. We have no further details at this time but I will take a few of your questions."

Pandemonium ensued as several reporters shouted all at once. Paul held up his hand and said, "One at a time! One at a time! You first, sir, in the blue jacket. State your name and your outfit."

"Joe Greeley, *New York Post*. If this is a triple homicide, was it a lovers' triangle gone wrong? "

"We are not aware of any inappropriate relationships among the victims. You, ma'am, in the hat."

"Annie McCarthy, *Hudson Register-Star*. If you have three killings on one night, is this the beginning of a serial killer?"

"No, we have no reason whatsoever to think that this is the work of a serial murderer. The deaths appear to be inter-related rather than random. You, sir."

"Raul Espinoza, *Variety*. Is Cassandra Chappelle the Broadway actress? Why was she up here? Was she teaching at Bard?"

"Ms. Chappelle had rented a vacation house outside of Rhinebeck. She underwrote the production but was not teaching at Bard. Last one, you, sir."

"Rudy Fennell, *Wall Street Journal*. Are these murders related to Franklin O'Connell's attempt to corner U.S. mining rights for rare earths?"

"Mr. O'Connell is fully cooperating with us on our investigation. We have no indication that these deaths have anything to do with him or his business affairs. That's it. Thank you."

Paul strode away as reporters hurled more questions after him. We got into a squad car and headed back to Bard.

Paul loosened his tie and leaning back against the seat, sighed.

"What a scene! Glad that's over."

"Yes, dear," I said. "Until the next one. And, may I also remind you, what winds up in the media after a press conference sometimes has less to do with your answers and more to do with the questions that you were asked."

True enough, the next day the papers were filled with speculation on a lovers' triangle ending in a triple homicide, the possibility that a serial killer was at large in the Valley, and a profile on Franklin O'Connell's suspiciously meteoric rise in various green energy industries.

Not surprising. Our leads hadn't produced any alternative assumptions or results as yet.

But annoying. Unless there was some tiny grain of truth tucked into those theories which we hadn't found. Yet.

RYAN'S COMPUTER REPORT

The next afternoon, we reconvened for Ryan's update on the computer and phone research.

"There's a lot of stuff," Ryan said. "I've gotten a new board to show you the connections I've found." He wheeled in a 4' x 8' blackboard and, picking up the chalk, started to outline the web of connections among the several suspects.

"Let's start with Palmer, the teacher from the drama department. He had emails, texts, and phone calls with almost every other person you are looking at.

"First, several with the dead kid's parents: The mother arranging to meet him for a conference. This was more than six months ago. The father arranging to drop by for coffee when he was in neighborhood for a business meeting, maybe a month back. Then a text asking about the time for the tech and dress rehearsal several days ago.

"Second, Palmer with the dead woman, Miss Chappelle. A few texts and emails, making three or four dates: Dinners or lunches, her coming to speak to his classes, conduct workshops. Her computer has the same stuff. Back and forth, a few times over several weeks."

"Third, with the dead boy. Rehearsal notes, *Henry V* script conferences, nothing really personal. The kid also replied, but sometimes not. The outreach was always from Palmer."

"What about with Eli, the roommate?" I asked.

Ryan consulted his notes. "Only a few but they were group emails about rehearsal times, notes on costume tweaks. They also went to several other students. I asked Win and Edwin"---he gestured to the officers---"about the names and

211

they confirmed that all of the other students in the email chains were also involved in the production."

"What about Big Ben?"

"A lot of texts from Mrs. O'Connell, mostly following up on meetings they'd had about his instructions for doing things around the property. Nothing useful on the night of the party."

"What else about Francesca O'Connell?" Paul asked.

"None from Donald Palmer, none from Brad Ruffin or his parents or from the girl, Eli Johnson. Ryan paused.

"What about between Louis Ruffin and the girl?"

Ryan consulted his notes. "They started being in touch a few months ago when she sent him a text from Brad's phone. It said, 'Brad is stuck in class. Come on over and we'll wait for him together.' There are other texts or her phone and his arranging to meet. In the evening, as a rule, but sometimes during the day."

"What else is on Brad's phone?" Paul asked. "Connections to Cassandra are what I'm interested in."

Ryan hesitated, then blushed. "I'd say they were lovers. At least he told her he loved her. And she told him back."

"No wonder Eli seduced his father!" I said. "She had access to Brad's phone---she'd seen those texts. She was livid!"

"I don't think you can claim the father is blameless in all of this," Paul snarled. "That letch. A real creep. When did they start getting together?"

Ryan consulted his notes. "A few months now. It started in the Spring."

Paul turned to Jackson and O'Reilly. "Something was driving him and I'm not sure it was just our old friend's lust. Get out to Connecticut and go through Ruffin's house and office. Find something that ties him into this mess! Find out if he knew her stepkids!"

THE KNOCK-OUT SPRAY REDUX

When Paul came into the incident room first thing the next morning, he found Ryan working industriously at the computer and me staring at the evidence boards trying to conjure up a theory on whether or not Eli would have killed Brad. I knew she could have, that she was angry and perhaps unstable.

"Have you found the records of the nerve gas purchase? That's what we need to tie the Chappelle thing up." Paul peered into the computer screen over Ryan's shoulder.

Ryan said, "No, sir. Can't find any on-line purchases for any kind of drug."

"Damn!" said Paul.

At that moment, Frank Carver made an unexpected but very timely appearance in the incident room.

"Anything here that passes for coffee?" he boomed out. "I didn't drive all the way to Bard College and not have anything to wash these down." He proffered a bakery box brimming with slices of pound cake and pastries.

"You've been to Le Perche!" I cried. That is our French bakery on Warren Street in Hudson. A few years ago, the owners shipped over a round brick oven from Normandy. The wood-fired monster is ten feet in diameter and cranks out sublime pastries and genuine baguettes. Divine.

Baked goods and a fresh pot of coffee distributed among Paul, the two sergeants, and me, Dr. Carver sat down and made his announcement.

"The Feds have gotten back to us on the chemical used to dispatch the unfortunate chef, the so called 'knock-out spray.' It was Fentanyl."

"Oh, God, not again!" Paul moaned. "We're seeing more and more of that junk up here. People are even lacing heroin with it."

Carver nodded. "Clandestine production has gotten hot as hell right now. Major problem with overdoses. The stuff is sold on the Deep Web and is well on its way to being a monster epidemic. But unless one of your suspects is selling it or buying it in quantity, getting large amounts on line to resell, or from a local dealer in volume, I'd say the better guess is that some doctor prescribed it."

Ryan interjected, "I know about that. My aunt had cancer. At the very end she wore Fentanyl patches on her arm. For pain. Had to be changed every 72 hours. You could take the transdermal patches," Ryan said, "and soak them in an alcohol/water solution. The liquid would leach out the chemical. If you did a whole box of them it would be a seriously lethal liquid."

"Which could be sprayed on a person," Paul and I said simultaneously. Crikey.

"Who would have written the Rx?" Jackson asked.

"How about that sleazeball Lothario, William Vance?" I suggested. "Somebody could have fed him some line, slipped him a few bucks. Although at this point, all we care about is proof of who bought it."

Paul turned to the deputies. "Go see Vance. Then get credit card statements. No, wait---this is faster. There's got to be a pharmacist who would remember that prescription. You two, call every pharmacy chain and independent between Albany and Poughkeepsie. See who has filled a prescription. Ask if it was Palmer, Eli Johnson, Ruffin, Francesca O'Connell, Big Ben, or either of those nitwits from Tenth Street. Call the NYC precinct and put them onto that, too. Damn! This is the link we've been waiting for."

The next day Sgt. Jackson rapped on the door frame.

"Come in, Win," Paul said. "What have you got?"

"You asked me to find out who sat next to the Ruffins at the play. The box office records showed two men were in the seats directly behind them, Frank Marion and Phil Faulkner. They live in Spencertown. Should I go and talk to them, sir?"

"Call them and tell them we are coming. You drive, Jackson. We'll all go. Let's get some fresh air."

Spencertown, so called because its early 19th century first settlers included twelve families named Spencer, is hardly more that a wide spot in the road and is a hamlet of Austerlitz, New York, a slightly wider spot in the road.

If you, like I, wonder how a town in upstate New York came to be named after Napoleon's most important victory, you need look no further than Martin van Buren, a Kinderhook native and favorite son of Columbia County.

Austerlitz was created in 1818 as an amalgam of parts of neighboring towns, Hillsdale, Chatham, and Canaan. At the creation of the new town, done to provide for closer oversight as the population grew, local German immigrants proposed calling the new town 'New Ulm,' recalling fondly a picturesque Southern village on the banks of the Danube.

The bill creating New Ulm passed the New York State Legislature and was sent to the Senate for confirmation. Martin Van Buren, then a State Senator and an ardent admirer of the great Napoleon---both were 5'6"---was still vexed that his political opponent Elisha Williams---6'1" and a devotee of Wellington---had succeeded in having a town near Rochester, New

215

York, christened 'Waterloo.' Van Buren suddenly leaped to his feet and moved to amend by calling the new town 'Austerlitz.' His motion carried, and he sat down, saying, 'There's an Austerlitz for your Waterloo.'

Those were the days, my friend.

Spencertown is essentially a collection of perhaps forty well-preserved 19th century houses on Route 203. Five Federal structures are listed in the National Register. There is also a general store. The hamlet's most famous resident was probably the late Ellsworth Kelly. I recently learned he was a great bird-watcher as a child; it is thought the number of two- and three-toned birds Kelly so fondly and frequently observed were a great influence on his color field paintings.

The Marion-Faulkner residence was a very handsome two-story clapboard Federal house, white with black shutters and a bright red door flanked by two pots of agapanthus in full bloom.

Serpentine boxwood hedges framed the front yard and three Leyland cypresses punctuated the slightly later north wing. Our knock on the door produced a tall, slender man with a tonsure of graying stubble, and a matching close-cropped beard. He wore frameless glasses, starched chinos, a gingham shirt, and had a gold watch chain attached to a belt loop and descending into his right pants pocket.

"You must be the sheriff," he said, smiling and holding the door open. "Although, with this many of you, I'd say you were possibly a posse! I'm Phil Faulkner, come on in."

After introductions in the foyer, he led us through the hall into a fine-looking, charcoal-painted parlor lined with bookcases, mirrors, beautiful paintings, and African sculptures and masks.

Faulkner said, "Keep walking, just through here. I thought we could sit out in the sunroom. It's almost like being

216

outside, but not so hot. Frank will be down in a minute, he's just showering."

The sunroom was long and narrow with windows facing a gravel courtyard and beyond that, gardens, lawn, a raised bed of tomato vines on conical trellises, Luytens benches, herbs in an eclectic collection of planters, and a beehive. We took seats on white slip-covered couches and chairs.

"Which of you called?" Faulkner asked.

"I called you, sir," answered Sgt. Jackson.

"You don't need to say 'sir,' " Faulkner laughed. "At my age, things are bad enough as it is. What can I help you with? You are asking about the *Henry V* production, right?"

"That's right," I answered.

"They took some liberties with the staging, but all in all, I'd say it was a very good production." He smiled. "But I'll bet you aren't here for my critique as a musician or theatre buff, right?"

A voice came through the louvered doors at the far end of the room.

"Where is everybody? I hate to be the last one at my own party! Oh, here you are."

"Here's Frank!" intoned Faulkner.

Frank Marion was a whippet-thin, also trimly bearded, also tonsured older man with a broad smile and strong, working man's hands. He wore tight white jeans and an olive drab military shirt, highly starched.

"I'm always saying I couldn't get arrested in this town but you may be about to prove me wrong! This place is awash in badges! I don't know whether to salute, pledge allegiance, or call Perry Mason! You all sit back down. What can we get you? Coffee? Too early for a Bloody?"

We demurred. I said, "Philip was just telling us about the evening you spent at *Henry V*. We are interested in the couple who sat in front of you."

"That was the damnedest thing. Do you remember, Philip? I told you something was wrong that night!"

"Wrong how?" asked Paul.

"Everything was fine for the first few scenes, we weren't even aware of the couple in front of us. Then when the battle started, with the lasers swinging around, lights flashing on stage, rear projection---great effects, by the way---the woman sort of slumped over and the husband started shaking her, whispering her name. Then he got up and quickly ran up the aisle toward the lobby, I figured to go get an usher to help him. Obviously something was the matter with her. He didn't come back, and didn't come back, then he finally showed up just as the battle ended. He'd brought her a glass of something, water, I guess. She sort of sat up, then leaned forward and held her head in her hands. He had his arm around her and was kissing her cheek. Then what happened, Philip?"

"Then the curtain fell. Then someone ran out from backstage and called for a doctor. Then the college president, Jason, came out and told us to go home, there was some sort of medical emergency. Then a woman seated several rows in front of us stood up, kind of screamed, and fell over. I guess dead."

◆◆◆◆◆

As we headed back to Hudson, Paul said, "Where do you suppose Ruffin went? Could he have had enough time to get to the stage? Knife the boy? Then get back to his seat? Before his wife came to and noticed he was AWOL?"

Sgt. O'Reilly, who was driving, spoke up.

"But, sir, even if he had time, he was in regular clothes. That would have given him away backstage. Everyone else was in costume."

Paul said, "Lindsey, remind us what were the soldiers wearing?"

"Most of them just tights and cloth tunics with a hood over their heads." I answered. Pondering Paul's hypothetical, I scowled, shaking my head.

"Good god! What a suggestion! How would he have had time? It's over a hundred yards to the stage door. True, tights and a muslin tunic would have fit under his clothes with no problem. But strip off, kill the kid, get dressed again? Somebody backstage would have noticed. And he could so easily have been observed in the lobby. There were ushers. The box office staff. An audacious idea, Paul! And furthermore, why kill his son?"

"Because the kid wasn't his damned son. He would have inherited his wife's money with the boy dead," Paul mused. "Maybe he planned to kill his wife next. He was sleeping with his son's girlfriend, don't forget."

"Well," I said, "I'll grant you he's a sleaze in good suits but you'll really have to lean on him to get any answers, much less an admission of guilt. Plus find the costume he wore. And find the weapon. I think your theory is extremely far-fetched, Paul. Just because he's a cad doesn't mean he's a murderer. And there isn't a shred of proof."

WHERE THERE'S A WILL

Sitting in the incident room, and staring at the walls and the boards of photographs, notes, and arrows and connecting dots, I kept saying to myself, 'motive, motive, motive.' What were the motives? Are the deaths connected? Who profits?

We still had no analysis of the Trenton and Baer purses.

Eli, it turned out, was a slightly medicated young woman, on anti-depressants. And, of course, grass. And too much alcohol. And the recent sedatives. Would she have been in such a fog, or gotten carried away by the action on stage, that she stabbed the boy?

Had I severely misjudged Francesca? She is not one to be crossed, that much was clear. A powerful, authoritative woman. But would she have killed to keep Franklin?

Was Palmer's grief at the boy's death genuine? Or was he purely the brilliant actor Jason described?

Stalking out into the sunshine, I got in my car and drove back to Cassandra's house. Exasperated, I stood in the middle of her office for what felt like the hundredth time.

I had gone through every drawer, every file, every cabinet and closet, as had Huxley, Paul, and several deputies.

None of us had found her will---and yet it had to be there.

I sat down again in the wing chair, propped my feet on the ottoman and gazed around the room.

Her file cabinets and desk? Ransacked.

Secret panels in the walls? All had been tapped.

False bottoms in any of the drawers? Nada.

Hollow books? All checked. Nothing.

Maybe the damned will was not in Cassandra's office after all but was stashed somewhere else.

I began to walk through Cassandra's house. Magda was bustling around, dusting, replacing dead flowers with fresh ones, pulling curtains aside to let in the morning light.

In the living room, a handsome walnut box I had not noticed before sat on the mantle. It looked like a reliquary.

"Magda, what is in that box?"

"Hashes."

"Pardon?"

"Mister Baxter's hashes."

"Do you have a key for it?" I asked.

"In de hottoman."

"Pardon?"

"In her hoffice!" she cried, annoyed with my incomprehension. "Der hassock! Vat to put your feet on. Der key to the hashes is in dere." She walked into the kitchen carrying vases as I headed back to the office.

I went back and stared at the ottoman. Huxley and I had already turned it upside down, poked its underside, and looked under its skirts. But Magda had said 'in the ottoman.'

Feeling around the sides of the chintz-covered top, my fingers found a metal knob. I pushed it, the top popped loose, and I lifted it. Beneath the top sat a recessed tray about twenty inches square.

A little gold key lay on top of a legal folder tied with a ribbon. I opened the folder and there lay Cassandra's will.

It was quite straightforward.

Every centime was left to Brad.

There was also a far more startling discovery which needed to go to Paul.

And quickly.

WHAT WAS REVEALED

"I found it!" I yelled as as I hurried back into the incident room.

"Found what?" Paul asked.

"I finally found Cassandra's bloody will. But I found a hell of a lot more than that."

I pulled out the legal folder.

"The document itself is straightforward. Every farthing at Cassandra's disposal was left to Brad. Her stepkids would have gotten a good deal of money because of their father's ironclad covenants in *his* will but the bulk of the estate was headed for Brad. But here's the other interesting thing I found."

I handed a sheet of paper to Paul.

"What the hell?!" He pulled off his glasses. "A marriage license! Between Brad and Cassandra! Good god! She was old enough to be his mother."

"So what?"

"It isn't natural…is it?" Paul winced.

"You men!" I snapped. "No one complains when a man dates a woman half his age. But, oh my! How the tongues wag when a *woman* seduces someone younger than she! Dear me! Robbing the cradle! You are not familiar with the term 'cougar' ? Think Annis/Fiennes or Moore/Kutcher. Madonna dates boys who are barely out of short pants, to say nothing of Phaedra, Catherine the Great, plus Elizabeth I *and* Elizabeth Taylor to name a few. Honestly!"

Men can be so exasperating.

WE NEED THE KNIFE

"What I'd like to know is why the hell we have no murder weapon yet?"

Paul's nerves were frayed and his temper was rising.

"Someone on that stage killed that boy. I want you two to go back to that Johnson girl's house, dismantle every cupboard, every drawer. Check the yard for recently disturbed soil. I also want Palmer's house, his yard, and his office searched again. Every nook, every cranny, every locker, book case, medicine cabinet, pantry, attic and cellar. I want the theatre gone over again. I want backstage dismantled. I'm going over to see how Hank is feeling after his surgery and bring him up to date and when I get back there better be some answers."

Paul stormed out.

Sergeants Jackson and O'Reilly and I looked at each other.

"Were the first searches as thorough as you could make them, sergeants?" I asked.

Both nodded.

"Lindsey, we had twenty people from both Hudson and the Rhinebeck police all over the theatre interior, the other spaces in the building, the theatre grounds, that house in Tivoli, and the teacher's office and his house at Bard. We found nothing," said Jackson.

"If I had stabbed someone," O'Reilly said, "I'd throw the damned knife in the River and no one would ever find it. That's likely what happened, and why we haven't found anything yet."

In my heart, I, too, worried that was what had happened, that we would never get that piece of evidence in our hands.

However, I am a believer in dogged persistence. What one may overlook on an initial search may be found on a second or third or fourth effort.

Putting my hands on the sergeants' shoulders, I tried to encourage them.

"We can't give up now, we are so close. Paul is depending on you. Sheriff Hank is depending on you. And I believe you can find that weapon. Go over Palmer's office and house and classrooms and the Spiegeltent and his dressing room in there *again*. Go back to the house in Tivoli. Either Palmer or the Johnson girl have to be the one who stabbed that kid. Go and find the knife.

"Remember lads, as Paul always says, 'It's not where you start, it's where you finish.' "

DEPUTIES' REPORT

Jackson and O'Reilly and their troops took Eli and Brad's house in Tivoli apart. They looked in eaves, crawled under the house, pulled up loose floorboards, moved appliances. They went over the front, side, and back yards with metal detectors.

They scoured Palmer's apartment looking for the knife but found nothing in any bookshelf, closet, drawer, chest, or armoire. All of the furniture was upended. They dismantled the desk and emptied every file.

They called to say they were on their way to Palmer's office.

Paul and I sat in the incident room combing through emails and texts to see if we had missed any significant connections or contradictions but we found nothing new.

At about five, Jackson burst in.

"I think we found it, sir!" he cried. "It was hanging right in front of us all along, in full view! There's a whole bunch of knives and blades arranged in a semi-circle-like on a wall in Palmer's office. This one was on the very end and I could see it was dirty."

"Show me!" Paul ordered.

Jackson unwrapped the ten inch package lying in his hand. It was a dagger. Persian? Greek? It had an ornate handle and a slightly curved blade. It was likely used in some play, one of the many theatrical props adorning Palmer's office.

"This looks to be traces of blood on the blade," Jackson said. "It hasn't even been wiped clean very well. I'm betting he used it to kill that boy, sir."

Paul looked at the knife and nodded slowly. He then broke into a big grin.

"I believe you have just cracked the case, Sgt. Jackson! Get this knife over to the lab, they'll have the boy's blood type. Have them match it to this. Have it done immediately and wait for the results. Call us here the second you have it. Now go, man!"

About an hour later, Jackson called to say the traces on the knife were blood matching Brad Ruffin's type.

I called the Drama department. The secretary said Palmer was at his apartment across campus.

"Let's go, Lindsey. We are making an arrest."

When we got there, Palmer was in his garden. He didn't seem surprised to see us.

Grabbing Paul's arm, I said, "Wait! Let me just have a word with him."

"Why?" Paul asked. "There is no way out."

Nodding, I said, "I know that, but let's at least give the man a chance to say what he needs to say. I'm sure he will confess. And that confession will make your life much easier."

Reluctantly, Paul agreed. "OK. Let's see if he comes clean."

We walked over and both sat down cross-legged on the grass next to Palmer.

"Hello, Don. What are you doing?" I asked.

"Dividing iris for an old friend." Palmer smiled.

"Huh! Lot of that going around. What friend is that?"

"Roberta Figgins."

"So she told you I went to see her."

Palmer nodded. He uprooted a clump of iris and began breaking the rhizomes apart.

"How are you and she connected?" Paul asked.

"I've known Berta for ages. She worked in costumes for years. She assistant stage-managed a couple of shows I was in, also had some minor roles. I thought she was a theatre lifer. But, some lover of hers asked her to help out at the adoption agency---and she found her true calling. Helping the waifs, the strays, the little lives that could so easily be lost, and matching them with people who wanted a child. Anyway, when Cassandra turned up 'in the family way,' as the euphemism of the day had it, she had no intention of keeping the child so I sent her to Roberta's office."

"Were you the father?" I asked.

"Possibly. Probably. Who knows?"

"But why murder?"

Throwing down his trowel, Palmer cried, "What choice did I have? Brad was about to throw his life away and I had to stop him! He had come to idolize Cassandra, he bought into her whole ridiculous song and dance. She told him they would travel the world, he would have the best drama coaches. That she *knew* people. That she could guide his career as no one else could. And she was still very beautiful. So beautiful."

Both deputies were walking towards us, O'Reilly with handcuffs out and ready. Paul motioned for them to hold up a few yards away.

"Don, please go on."

Tears began to roll down his cheeks.

"I tried to explain to Brad that any connections Cass had to the theatre were long gone, and, at any rate, no one's first role in classical theatre is as the leading man. But all he could see was his name in lights---next to hers.

"I know how he felt. I know how easily she seduced men. I was in love with her myself all those years ago. She promised me we'd do the big time together, we'd double bill on the great white way. But she never cared for anyone but herself. And for men who could further her career.

"When Brad told me they were going to be married, that he had actually proposed, I told him he was out of his mind. And so was she! Of course, she didn't know who he was," he said bitterly.

"But I did. Roberta had told me years ago when she placed him with the Ruffins. But suppose someday *Brad* figured it out? I begged him to stop seeing her! I begged him! But he laughed at me. I had to stop him. I had to! He couldn't be allowed to go through with it!

"Can you imagine how the poor bastard would feel if he found out that he had married his own mother?"

"But murder, Don?"

"Yes! Murder! Murder!" he cried. "I couldn't figure out any other way to stop him, to stop their marriage."

"But he was so young, Don. There must have been another way. You didn't have to kill him."

"What?" Palmer choked out the word through his tears.

"I said, 'You didn't have to kill him.' "

"Christ, I didn't kill *him*. I killed *her*."

It isn't easy to see a man's life in ruins.

Palmer's face was a tragic mask but it was eerily calm.

Paul and I sat with him in an interview room at the Hudson Sheriff's department, a gray-walled 15 by 15 box with a two-way mirror on one wall, four metal chairs and a bare table.

"Take us through it, Don," Paul said. "Did Vance give you the Fentanyl scrip?"

He nodded.

"I thought the poison was fitting," Palmer said, with a wry half-smile.

"So many conspicuous, marvelous historical references. Cleopatra, Madame Bovary. Cassandra went like other great heroines. She had to be sacrificed.

"But Brad is the tragedy! How could I have known Brad would die? Why? Why? That beautiful boy..."

Still staring at us, he began to weep.

"All for nothing. Nothing."

"You only pretended to leave the O'Connells' " I said. "Then you doubled back and found the chef outside."

"Yes."

"Suppose he hadn't been outside?" Paul asked. "What was your plan then?"

Wiping away his tears, Palmer cleared his throat.

"Stagecraft! As always! I slapped on a beard and a wig I had hidden in my jacket. I planned to go in, find the chef, lure him out, explain that some problem needed his attention. That was my plan. Then knock him out, make the substitution on the salad and leave. He'd never have been able to identify me. But when I came around the side of the house, I found him outside, having a cigarette. I asked him for a light, sprayed him with the Fentanyl, and threw him in the shrubbery. But he didn't stay down! So I gave him another huge dose and decided to be safe, I'd drag him down to the boathouse. He got up again and tackled me so I grabbed a boat gaff and hit him with it. He fell against a dinghy. I put him in a rigging bag to keep him out of my way. I had no idea he was dead until you found him a few days later. At that point, Brad was dead and I was past caring about anything."

Paul said, "You're going to need an attorney but we can take care of that tomorrow before your arraignment."

As Paul and I stood to leave, Palmer said, "May I ask a question?"

"What is it, Don?" I asked.

"Where will she be buried?"

THE MURDER WEAPON AND OTHER MATTERS

When I came in first thing the next morning with a heavy heart, bearing orange juice, and so miserable about poor, deranged Palmer I thought of also bringing a flask of vodka, I found Paul and his two sergeants pacing back and forth muttering to themselves.

Responding to their agitation, I said, "Shouldn't you be slightly happy? You found Cassandra's killer and you found the knife that dispatched Brad. Progress, gentlemen! Progress!"

Paul shook his head.

"We accidently found Chappelle's murderer and we found the knife that killed Brad Ruffin, but not his killer. God, I hate this case."

Jackson spoke up, "Sir, I've just been on the phone with the lab. There was one other thing they found about the knife from Palmer's office that's kind of odd."

"Odd? Odd how?" Paul asked.

"The blade had the kid's blood all over it but the hilt had been wiped clean. Or, at any rate, had no fingerprints at all."

"So why leave the blood but wipe the hilt? Or maybe gloves..." Paul, too, began to stride around the room, lost in thought. Suddenly he stopped and cried, "It's a set up. The knife was planted back in Palmer's office after the murder. But who, damn it!?"

We hurried over to the drama department and spoke to Millie, the secretary whose desk sits outside Palmer's office. I knew from earlier conversations that she was a sweetheart. She also turned out to be a stickler for details.

I asked, "Millie, do you keep a log of who visits the department, say, parents who come for conferences, students, other visitors?"

"I certainly do. Faculty evaluations include their being available to parents and students, so I keep track of that. Also, we have a fair number of maintenance calls---air conditioning or heat, internet, and so forth, so I want to be able to confirm those visits occurred in case anyone should ask. I started out here in bookkeeping so I guess I got into the habit of keeping records." She smiled at us, eyebrows up, waiting.

"May we see your log?" I asked, expecting her to pull out some sort of ledger.

"It would be easier if you came around here," she said, motioning Paul and me to stand beside her so we could see her computer monitor. She opened an Excel file with every visitor catalogued by date and time.

"What are you looking for?" she asked.

"Palmer's visitors during the week before *Henry V.* And in the days just after," Paul said.

"This is about that poor young man, isn't it?" she said, flicking a few keys.

"Yes, all right. Let's see." Millie began to scroll down.

"Here's the week before the performance. Dr. Priestly a few times. Several sets of parents. Let's see...mother and father from Indiana, father from Florida, mother from Virginia. About a dozen students taking summer classes had appointments. A few junior faculty came for regularly scheduled meetings. And there's a full drama staff meeting every Wednesday morning. Usually lasts about an hour."

"What about his student, Eli Johnson?" I asked.

"No...no..."---Millie continued scrolling---"don't see her name. Here's another parent, the boy's father, Louis Ruffin. He was here the Tuesday before the performance. Spent about half an hour. Then…let's see…he popped in last Sunday to return some books he had borrowed."

"Was Palmer in his office when Ruffin stopped by that Sunday?"

"No, he wasn't. That was just after you two," gesturing to Paul and me, "had been in to see Don, the morning after that terrible accident on stage. Don left shortly after you met with him, told me he was going home, to compose himself, I'd say. He was terribly upset about that boy's death."

Paul impulsively kissed Millie on the top of her head and yelled, "Thanks!" as we all tore down the stairs and out onto the Quad. Our urgency and sense of dread felt bizarre as we found ourselves among students throwing Frisbees, strumming guitars, or lounging on the green reading on a beautiful summer afternoon.

Paul said, "Ruffin showed up on Sunday to put the knife back on Palmer's wall. We have to find him."

I called Dottie's cell but got no answer.

Paul put out an APB with the license plates of Ruffin's car. The sergeants began calling the Madalin hotel as well as Ruffin's home and office.

Suddenly, from far across the quad, a figure ran toward us screaming, "Help me! Help her! Please help! Help!"

Eli Johnson reached us, gasping, and lunged at me and Paul.

"It's Brad's mother! It's Dottie! Louis has her!" she cried.

"Where are they?" Paul cried.

"In the Spiegeltent! Hurry! Hurry!"

The five of us sprinted across the green.

Inside the tent, rows of klieg lights and spots were revolving, flashing off and on.

In the middle of the performance area, in the center of the dance floor, Dottie lay crumpled and unmoving as Louis Ruffin paced around her, waving his arms and screaming, "You would leave me?! Never!" He held a prop spear in one hand and a pistol in the other.

"Ruffin!" Paul shouted. "No point in hurting her. Put your gun down. It's over. Let's talk."

Ruffin screamed, "I'll say when this is over!"

Sgt. Jackson had entered the tent several steps behind us. He darted quickly behind a row of palms along the perimeter of the tent. Crouching, he began to inch slowly toward the stage, staying down and out of sight.

Giving his wife a vicious shove with his foot, Ruffin ranted on.

"I've been shafted my entire life! Franklin O'Connell screwed me out of a fortune and there was nothing I could do. My wife is the one with the money, that frigid bitch. And then I find she's leaving everything to that sorry bastard who isn't even my son! I won't be replaced by some faggot boy! And I won't be divorced!"

Eli screamed, "He's not a faggot!"

"And you!" Ruffin screamed at Eli. "You were my last hope! I thought you cared! I thought you wanted me!"

Paul and I exchanged nervous glances. This could end very badly. Under my breath, I said to Eli, "You're an actress. Talk to him. Humor him. Distract him."

"Louis," she began, walking slowly toward him.

"Oh, Louis! Please stop this! You haven't done anything yet, not really! Please let Dottie go. You and I can explain to these people. Tell them this is all a mistake! You never intended to hurt her! You're just upset! Please stop!"

Ruffin's arms fell to his sides.

"I could stop if I thought you wanted me, that you weren't just using me. Show me. Show me now!" He held out a hand to Eli. "Come here, darling Eli! Kiss me!"

Paul and I looked at each other. This was not a good development.

Eli looked scared but she began to move slowly toward Ruffin.

"Louis, you know I love you. Please stop. I'm coming to show you!"

As she reached Ruffin, he took her arm and brutally jerked her toward him, spun her around and hooked his arm around her throat, pulling her close to him.

We saw Jackson for half a second as he edged around a bank of lights and eased himself onto the stage behind Ruffin.

Ruffin's face twisted into a terrifying grimace. "Now I have you both! I'm going to finish this!" He brandished the gun and placed it against Eli's temple.

"Ruffin! Look at me!"

The shout came from the stage as Jackson hurtled through the air and tackled Ruffin from behind, tearing his arm away from Eli. The men began to struggle but Jackson's hard right cross stopped that and he knelt astride Ruffin with a foot on the gun as the rest of us moved in.

"Cut those damned strobes!" I shouted and O'Reilly rushed to find the breakers.

As Ruffin was hand-cuffed, read his rights, and taken away, Paul, Eli, and I knelt by Dottie, helping her sit up, softly whispering reassurances to her. She gradually came around.

"What happened?" Her voice was very weak. "I don't remember anything after Louis asked me to meet him here. He caught me at the door, slapped me, dragged me in, and there were all these flashing lights. I blacked out right away. Has anyone been hurt? Eli, why are you crying? Come here, sweetie." And the two women embraced.

◆◆◆◆◆

That evening, Ruffin confessed to the whole sorry story.

Arrogant even in defeat and disgrace, he emphasized his cleverness in crafting the tunic costume from a length of muslin.

He was very proud of his athleticism and his split-second timing, racing out of the theatre as the battle began, knowing his wife would have become a zombie, sprinting along the side of the theatre while tearing off his tuxedo and stashing it in some shrubbery, knifing his son amid the melee onstage, darting back out the stage door, pulling the tux back on over his tunic, returning the knife to the pocket inside his jacket, then rejoining Dottie at his seat.

When we retrieved his tux, Brad's blood was on the lining of the coat.

When Paul asked him why, Ruffin simply said, "I had planned everything about my life so carefully. Very carefully. But I'd gotten some bad breaks. It was time for my luck to change.

"I had to try a new strategy, speed things up. I wanted the money that should have been mine all along. I was ready for a new life. I was ready for a new wife. And I only needed nine minutes."

BACK TO WHAT PASSES FOR NORMAL

Bennett had made a beautiful salmon and a heavenly cream sauce with shallots and masses of tarragon.

I don't want to remember this luncheon as a post mortem, so grim, but I suppose it was.

Everyone involved---let's not call them the usual suspects---sat on my porch and watched the river gliding by. The Casa Blanca lilies in the garden were six feet tall and they, along with the early autumn clematis, in full battle array climbing up onto the porch railings, bathed us in fragrance. The cachepots were overflowing with white New Guinea impatiens and cerise geraniums. The croquet course was set and waiting.

We were eight.

Franklin and Francesca sat together on the settee.

Bennett sat between Dottie and Eli.

Huxley was arrayed sideways in the hammock.

Paul and I sat in chairs opposite each other.

Huxley, on his fourth glass of Champagne, was toasting Cassandra.

"She may have thought *Harlot* was her finest role, but I think her death scene in *Henry V* is what she'll be remembered for!"

"That's a hell of a thing to say, Huxley! Jesus!" I snapped.

"Don't snap at me, youngish lady! You did not have drinks with Dr. Carver two days ago. He shared with me a little nugget from Cassandra's autopsy."

Paul's eyebrows shot up.

"Now, sheriff, calm down. It wasn't relevant to Cassandra's death and Frank was only seeking to console me--- he knew Cass was my friend. But, the fact is, she had a big aneurism on the top of her little head. Inoperable, could have popped any minute. This was a much more dramatic way to go---and Bard got the underwriting in the meantime!"

Somewhat mollified, Paul said, "We had a lot of good teamwork on this, even you helped, Smythe, and we thank you. The Dutchess county sheriff is back now. Hank's commended Jackson and O'Reilly for their initiative and bravery."

He stopped for a moment. Then turning to Francesca with a wry smile, Paul said, "Mrs. O'Connell, I hope you realize we were just doing our jobs. For the record, I want you to know that Lindsey never went along with your being a suspect for one minute. Never. But, you must admit, the evidence against you looked very strong. We couldn't ignore it. But I'm glad I was wrong."

He raised his glass to her.

Bennett asked, "And how are you, Dottie?"

"There is no point in saying that my heart is not broken," Dottie answered in a sad voice. She stood and walked over to the railing, the River behind her.

"I loved Brad. But sometimes children lose their way. And perhaps he was saved from a disastrous future. Who can know? Louis did not seem insane when we married but I think I never really understood how deeply he resented my money---and the way he internalized every business slight, making it a personal vendetta. That destroyed him. His ambition consumed him. But now, I have to try to move on with my life."

Franklin said, "I swear to you, Dottie, I never set out to ruin Louis. He was ahead of the market and he didn't understand that the numbers simply didn't work. I even offered him a position with our firm---but he wanted to be a managing partner or nothing. He was in too much of a hurry."

He turned to Francesca and took her hand.

"As a man gets older, sometimes he starts to wonder if he took all his shots, if the status quo isn't too pat. Oh, hell, why try to explain it. There's no fool like an old fool. Thank God for my wife's understanding. And patience."

Francesca, lovely in pale blue linen, beamed at him, and at all of us, when she answered, "Oh, Franklin. What marriage doesn't have its ups and downs? My darling, we have each other, always will, there's nothing to worry about. All of this is behind us. Except for this."

She pulled a length of piano wire from her purse.

Dottie said, "There is one good thing to come out of this sorry mess."

She slipped her arm around Eli's shoulder.

"I've always wanted a daughter. And now I believe I have her."

"Croquet, anyone?" I asked.

Made in the USA
Middletown, DE
25 October 2018